I SAW YOU!

IT WAS AS IF SOMEONE HAD TURNED ON A shower of ice water over Jack's head. He clenched his jaw so hard his teeth ground.

"You saw me?" he echoed, trying to make the statement sound absurd. "Saw me what?"

"Saw you with Jill. I saw you come in. And I saw you leave. I saw you."

"I don't know what you're talking about."

"Jack and Jill went up the hill . . ."

"Don't sing anymore, Martin, I'm serious."

Okay, so he saw me, Jack was thinking, trying to stay calm. He still had nothing to worry about. Nothing. Nothing . . .

Martin crossed and uncrossed his legs. He looked at the ground and spoke even more softly and almost sadly. "You're mad at me, aren't you?"

The question took Jack by surprise, but in a way, it pleased him, too. So that's what this was all about. Crazy kid. It was just an excuse to get Jack to talk to him. He felt the old guilt rumbling. "Mad at you? Don't be absurd. Mad at you for what?"

"Yes, you are. You're mad at me. You don't like me. Nobody likes me. I know."

NURSERY CRIMES

JACK AND JILL

BY ERIC WEINER

HarperPaperbacks
A Division of HarperCollinsPublishers

HarperPaperbacks *A Division of* HarperCollins*Publishers*
10 East 53rd Street, New York, N.Y. 10022

Copyright © 1995 by Creative Media Applications, Inc. All rights reserved. No part of this book may be used or reproduced in any manner whatsoever without written permission of the publisher, except in the case of brief quotations embodied in critical articles and reviews. For information address HarperCollins*Publishers*, 10 East 53rd Street, New York, N.Y. 10022

Series created by Creative Media Applications, Inc. and Eric Weiner.
A Creative Media Applications Book.
Editor: Susan Freeman

Cover illustration by Danilo Ducak

First HarperPaperbacks printing: February 1995

Printed in the United States of America

HarperPaperbacks and colophon are trademarks of HarperCollins*Publishers*

❖ 10 9 8 7 6 5 4 3 2 1

Jack and Jill went up the hill,
To fetch a pail of water;
Jack fell down, and broke his crown,
And Jill came tumbling after.

Then up Jack got and off did trot,
As fast as he could caper,
To old Dame Dobb, who patched his nob
With vinegar and brown paper.

"I'VE GOT IT ALL WORKED OUT," JACK SAID. He grinned, but his heart was pounding. "I found a place," he explained. "You know . . . where we can be alone."

It was November, a gray blustery afternoon. Eighteen-year-old Jack Washburn III was standing with his beautiful girlfriend, Jill, on one of the dreary slate paths of the main quad of Braddington Prep.

Braddington was one of New England's richest and most exclusive private schools. It was also among the strictest. Girls and boys were not allowed in each other's dorms—ever.

Jill was studying his face, waiting. "Where?"

"I thought you'd never ask." Jack took Jill's fluffy pink-mittened hand in his. He took a breath. "My room," he said.

He saw the flash of alarm in her large green eyes.

"If you don't want to, I'll understand, but I've been working on this plan for a couple of weeks. It's all set up and—"

"Yes," Jill said.

"Yes what?"

"Yes I'll sneak into your room."

"Yes?"

Jill nodded.

"Yes!"

Jill started laughing. But just then, the school bell began its deep mournful chime . . . one . . . two . . .

It was time.

"Okay," Jack said, taking her arm, "we're going to have to move fast."

Even though the quad was deserted, Jack leaned forward and whispered in Jill's ear.

Jill nodded several times, her face grave.

Jack stepped back.

And then both he and Jill turned abruptly and walked in separate directions, as if they were strangers.

VIII

CHAPTER 1

BRADDINGTON PREP WAS AN OLD SCHOOL, ONE of the oldest in the country. The founding date, 1821, was right there on the coat of arms the academy printed on all its mugs and T-shirts and sweatshirts and notepads. Jack's dorm, Whitman Hall, was one of the oldest buildings on campus. So was nearby Franklin House. The two dorms were built the same year, 1893—long before they admitted girls into the school.

Obviously, the architect hadn't worried when he connected the two dorms with a basement passageway.

The connecting door was kept locked at all times, of course. And only Jack's dorm head, Mr. Simmons, had the key. But every Monday night, Mr. Simmons met with his senior dorm proctor, Cameron Kraft, to discuss rules and infractions by students. Like Jack, Cameron was a varsity wrestler. He was also one of Jack's best friends. And at his last Monday meeting, Cameron had stolen the key. Jack had copied it. Step one.

Jill was a day student. It would have looked suspicious

for her to hang out in Franklin House all by herself. So Jack had arranged for Jill to go visit Cameron's girlfriend, Brooke Swanson. Step two. Brooke would take Jill down to the Franklin basement smoking room and—

Jack checked his Rolex as he strode into Whitman: 2:16. He and Jill had seventh period free; most kids had class or gym at the end of the day. Jack knew he could count on the dorm to be almost deserted. He hurried past the common room to the stairs and started down.

Strange shapes loomed in the dark basement. Along with the boiler and the maze of padded pipes, the dusty room was filled with bicycles and boxes, Mr. Simmons's kayak, and all the other kinds of junk the students stored down here. There was a small utility room off the main space, which the students had decorated and Simmons had designated as the smoking room—for seniors only. Jack stuck his head in. Empty.

Before he had left to meet Jill in the quad, Jack had cleared a few boxes out of the way, making a path to the connecting door, along the back wall. Now his hand trembled as he fished out the key. He had already tried it once. He knew it worked. Still, he was suddenly convinced it wouldn't work *now*.

The truth was, a small part of him *hoped* it wouldn't work. Because if Jill was caught with even one foot inside Whitman, it meant automatic expulsion for them both. And *that* would mean—

No, no, he couldn't think about that *now*.

Besides, they wouldn't get caught.

The basement door was old and battered. Jack fit the key in the lock but didn't turn it. He waited. A moment later he heard a soft rap on the door that made his heart pound.

2

He glanced back at the empty basement, double-checking that he was alone. Then he unlocked the door and pulled it open. The door scraped noisily against the cement floor. And—

There stood Jill, like a vision.

She had taken off her green overcoat. Underneath, she was wearing a black cable-knit sweater that made her strawberry-blond hair look even more lustrous and shiny than usual.

Behind Jill stood Brooke, half-turned so she could watch the hallway and make sure Mrs. Wallace, Franklin House's dorm mistress, didn't suddenly start down the basement steps on the girls' side.

Jack felt like he was in a dream. Jill seemed to be appearing from a cloud, as opposed to a dusty basement.

He stepped aside. "Come on," he whispered.

It was the point of no return.

She walked in.

Nodding to Brooke, Jack closed and locked the door. Then he shoved a few boxes back into place. Grabbing Jill's hand, he hurried them through the basement and up the stairs. As they reached the first landing Jack saw that—

Someone had wedged open the stairwell door.

Jack felt sick. He could hear the sound of cartoons drifting out of the common room, and through the open doorway, he caught a glimpse of somebody's scuffed boots resting on the coffee table.

He took a firm grip of Jill's arm. They kept walking, past the open door, climbing the steps. Not running, but almost.

Halfway up the first flight of stairs, Jill stumbled, her foot slipping off the edge of the stone step. Jack held her up. Otherwise, she would have fallen hard. They kept going.

Second floor.

3

Suddenly Jack felt a strong, almost overpowering urge to turn back. His knees felt weak. But turning back now might be even more dangerous than going ahead.

Third floor.

Jack opened the door on the third-floor landing. "Here," he said. His voice came out all raspy.

Jack's room was the first on the right. The first door on the left was a closed door, 3-H. As usual, the lights in 3-H were out, the tiny peephole was dark. And just then, Jack froze.

It wasn't that it was unusual for 3-H to be closed. While most kids kept their doors open during the day, crazy Martin Rucker kept his door closed at all times.

It wasn't unusual. It was just . . .

Silently pushing himself to keep moving, Jack forced the worry from his mind.

He had left his door unlocked. He always did. It was sort of a badge of honor. He liked the idea that he had nothing to hide. Truth was, as captain of the wrestling team, he was one of the few kids in Whitman who didn't have to worry about anyone trashing his room. He swung the door open for Jill and motioned for her to go in first. Then he glanced down the empty hallway, left, right. No one. He stepped in after her and closed the door. This time he locked it.

Then he turned.

He had a senior suite, one large living room with a little bedroom through the archway. He had fixed up the room nicely, with fancy modern furniture; framed posters; two standing halogen lamps; a wall unit loaded with sports trophies and state-of-the-art electronic equipment; a rolltop desk; a water bed (the school's lousy desk and cot were stored in the basement); and a huge yellow-and-blue parachute, which he'd hung from the ceiling like a canopy.

4

Just in case Jill had agreed to sneak in, he had cleaned carefully this afternoon, putting out a tennis can with a single long-stem red rose. He had left the shades all the way down, shutting out the bright afternoon sun that glared so brightly off the snow. The steam was hissing wildly in the old radiators. Jill was standing in the middle of the room, just standing there, staring at him, and looking totally out of place.

"We did it," Jack said quietly.

Jill was apparently too nervous to answer. She grinned a jagged lopsided grin.

Jack ripped off his black woolen topcoat and tossed it on the sofa. "It's okay, Jill. We're fine now. We're safe."

Safe. At the moment, thought Jack, safe seemed like an alien concept.

"Oh, wow, Jack." Jill laughed, sounding a little hysterical. "That was intense."

"I know."

"We're crazy, Jack."

"No, we're not. It's this school that's crazy. Look at us. So scared to go into a room together! This place turns you into criminals."

Jill was slowly beginning to thaw. She looked around the room for the first time, turning slowly. "So this is where you live," she said shyly.

"Yeah. Pretty nice, huh?"

Dumb thing to say, Jack told himself. Jack was a millionaire, or would be, when he turned twenty-one and collected on his trust fund. Jill's family was dirt poor. She was on full scholarship. What was he trying to do? Rub it in?

Jill ran her finger over the computer keyboard. Thanks to a rich alumnus, Braddington had installed a computer system, with a terminal in every room, complete with modems connecting them with

Internet. Jack had left the terminal booted up; part of an essay for English class was still on the screen, the little white cursor winking. Jill looked down at the keyboard and with one forefinger tapped out HI.

Jack smiled. Just then the computer beeped twice and an E-mail note popped into view. Jill laughed when she read it. He moved closer, peering over her shoulder.

HEY, DOG BREATH. YOU GOT ANY MORE OF THOSE BROWNIES?

"It's from Hunt," Jack explained. "He's always netting me."

"You guys have all the fun," Jill said.

Hunt Lowry was another one of Whitman's varsity wrestlers. He lived just six doors down the hall.

"There's no chance . . . ?" Jill began.

"That Hunt'll come over?" Jack answered. "Nah. And if he does, we just won't answer."

Jill nodded tensely.

They had always been so easy with each other, right from that first day when Jill happened to fall in behind him on line in the cafeteria. He had advised her to take the pizza instead of the hamburgers, which had blobs of gray mucusy grease on them. Not a very tough choice, but it had started the conversation going, and then he had followed her to her table without even asking. They ended up talking all through lunch just as naturally as if they'd been friends for months.

But now, alone together like this, Jack suddenly felt awkward, as if this were a blind date.

Jill kept looking around the room and—"Oh, Jaaaack!" She had seen the rose. "That was so sweet of you. " Her eyes were sparkling.

He took a step toward her. She took a step away. She studied some of the objects on his mantel, touched the dimpled leather skin of the football.

6

"My most valuable possession. That's a real Superbowl game ball," Jack said. "Look, it's autographed by Troy Aikman. He gave it to me personally, right after the game. My dad knows the Cowboys' owner."

"Oh," said Jill. She put the football back on the mantel. It started to roll off, and she had to snap her hand back up to hold the ball in place.

"I worship Troy Aikman, by the way," Jack said.

"Really? That's so cute."

She picked up the plastic snow-globe souvenir he had bought the last time he went skiing in Vermont. Her hand was trembling, swirling up a little of the toy's plastic snowflakes. She shook the toy hard, making it snow down on the tiny chalet inside.

"I collect those," Jack said.

"You do? But . . . I only see one."

"I just started the collection."

Normally Jill would have laughed at that, but now she only smiled. Well, she wasn't the only one who was tense. His voice was shaking.

She shook the bauble again. "Cute," she said. "*Cute!* Listen to me! I'm calling everything cute. When your dorm head bursts in and catches us, I'll probably tell him he's cute, too."

"The door's locked."

She turned. He had cornered her again, with her back to the mantel. But it was as if there was an invisible barrier between them, and he was afraid to cross it. She was looking down at the floor. Something sparkled around her neck.

"I've been meaning to ask you," he said softly. He reached his hand partway toward her. "What's—"

"This?" She held up the silver tear-shaped pendant. "Present from my dad. Sweet sixteen."

"Can I?"

7

Pause. She nodded.

He held it in his hand, turning it over gently. This brought their heads closer together, by at least an inch.

"It's beautiful," he said.

"Thanks. I wear it all the time."

"*All* the time?"

"Uh huh. In the shower, to sleep—always."

His heart had begun pounding so hard he was afraid she would hear it. She caught the look in his eye. Something was passing back and forth between them. Words without words. Abruptly, she reached behind her neck with both hands. Jack was so excited, he thought he was going to faint. Without taking her eyes off his, Jill unclasped the necklace and set it down on the mantel.

The football rolled off the shelf and thumped around the floor. They didn't pay any attention.

Jill's bare neck with the little hollow where the pendant had nestled—it struck Jack as the most breathtaking sight he'd ever seen.

It was dark in the room. He could hear her breathing. He could see the tiny dark flecks in her green eyes. As he bent his head down to kiss her, he saw her pupils dilate.

He kissed her neck first. Then worked his way back up.

It wasn't their first kiss—not by a long shot; ever since they'd started going out in September, they'd been making out every chance they got. It wasn't a long kiss either—maybe five, six seconds tops.

But it was pure magic.

It was like, after the kiss, they could both breathe again. As if the invisible barrier that had come between them was gone again.

Jill seemed to crumple against him as he wrapped

his arms tightly around her. She rested her head against his shoulder. He squeezed her tightly. He almost felt like crying. They had done it! They had done it! He had snuck her in—easy as pie.

Just like he had told her, thought Jack as they swayed back and forth in each other's arms.

Nothing could go wrong.

It was a perfect plan.

CHAPTER 2

THREE HOURS LATER . . .

Jack was walking back from the third-floor bathroom with a towel over his shoulder, a toothbrush in his mouth, and his white ceramic Braddington mug in his hand. Despite the toothbrush, he was singing—belting out Nirvana's "Smells Like Teen Spirit."

He had left his room wide open. He slapped his mug down on his desk. Then he heard someone clear his throat. He turned, surprised.

Cameron was sitting in the wing chair, his Air Jordans resting on the glass coffee table.

Cameron grinned. "So . . . how did it go?"

"Like clockwork."

"Really? Sounds kinky."

"Oh, I thought you meant sneaking in." Jack shut his door. "I'm not talking about anything else."

"C'mon. . . ."

"No."

"Then it's serious."

"What are you talking about?"

10

"You told me about all the others. If you don't want to talk about it, it means you're in love."

Jack was perfectly willing to admit it. He felt like it was written all over his face anyway. "All right, then I'm in love."

Cameron was tall and thin with a year-round tan. His blond hair was shockingly yellow and he wore it parted in the middle in a ridiculous haircut that only someone as good-looking as Cameron could have pulled off. Cam was one of the smartest kids Jack had ever met. With his wire-rim glasses, he even looked smart.

"C'mon, tell me," Cameron said.

"No way. You'll have to find another way to get your cheap thrills. Like with Brooke."

Cameron frowned. "We're through."

"Oh, I forgot," said Jack, slapping his forehead. "It's an odd-numbered day."

Cameron and Brooke broke up and got back together so often it was impossible to keep track of when it was on and when it was off. Even Brooke and Cam never seemed to know.

"Sure, you can make fun," said Cameron. "You've got your townie princess."

"Don't call her that."

"Jack . . . don't go all politically correct on me, would ya? She lives in town. She's a townie. End of story. No offense."

"Okay. No offense taken."

"So it's serious, huh?"

"Apparently."

Cameron whistled. "Can you imagine what your parents would do if you ever like married her or something? Wouldn't that be a kick in the pants!"

"Why?"

"Oh, come on, Jack. Don't be naive. Money marries

money, you know that. Filthy-rich kid marries townie? This is a headline, Jack."

"We're not getting married, Cameron. I snuck her into my room. That's all."

Jack picked a bag off his desk and tossed it to Cameron, who caught it with one hand.

"I don't want taffy," Cameron said. "I'm sick of taffy. When are you going to get some new junk food around here?"

Jack opened a drawer and stared down into it. "Blue corn tortilla chips, only one week old?"

Cameron yawned. "I'm going back to my room. I've got to crack that English book Percy gave us. Listen, if you decide to get real and divulge some juicy details, come find me, wouldya?"

"Deal."

Cameron stood up and did a funny shuffling two-step toward the door. Jack laughed. Tonight, everything was striking him as wonderfully hysterical. He knew why, too. Jill.

"Hey, Cam . . ."

Cameron had opened the door. He turned back. "Yeah?"

"You sure you don't want to talk about Brooke?"

"Defo."

"It's just that she's crazy for attention, you know. That's all it is."

Cameron shrugged. He wasn't talking tonight. This much was clear. And the truth was, despite Jack's reputation among his friends for being a natural-born shrink, tonight he only wanted to talk to Jill. Tonight, the eight-o'clock check-in rule that he had lived with for five years seemed barbaric to him. He longed to sneak out and race to her. But then again, taking two bonehead risks in one day—that was what was known as pushing one's luck.

He flopped down on the water bed, covering his eyes with one forearm. There was a knock at the door.

"I knew you'd come around, Cam," Jack said. "Have a seat. The doctor is in."

His visitor coughed politely. Jack took his arm down, then sat up.

"Martin!" he said. He grinned. "He lives!"

Standing in the doorway was a short, stoop-shouldered boy in an ill-fitting, three-piece gray suit.

"Hey there, Jack," Martin said; his voice, as always, was soft as a whisper. "You busy?"

Jack had about an hour's worth of studying to do. He didn't feel like doing it at the moment (he didn't feel like studying ever again, unless he was studying Jill), but he also didn't feel like talking to Martin. He was feeling so high; Martin was almost always a downer.

Jack felt a pang of the old guilt. It was always there. Right below the surface. "Not busy for you," he said with a wink.

Martin smiled briefly. "Oh, that's nice, Jack, that's nice of you to say."

Martin stayed in the doorway, awkwardly leaning against the jamb, looking at Jack as if he were waiting for something. Jack realized what.

"Oh, come in, come in," Jack told him.

There was no other kid in all of Whitman Hall, not even among the first formers, who was as polite or formal as Martin Rucker. The guy's father was some big-shot diplomat or something. He'd been ambassador to China for a while and had received a lot of credit for brokering some peace treaty between two warring countries in Central Africa. As for Martin, the kid was supposed to be some kind of genius. Whatever. He spoke and acted in this overly careful

13

manner that made him seem like a young British butler. Which was particularly odd for Rucker; with his slight frame and pale baby face, Martin looked more like twelve than seventeen.

Jack gestured to the wing chair. "Have a seat."

Martin sidled into the room. Sat. He crossed his legs, lacing his thin dainty fingers across one knee. Jack sat on his desk, waiting. But Martin just stared off into space as if he were alone.

"Taffy?"

"Oh, yes, thanks, Jack."

"You're sitting on them."

"I'm what? Oh, yes I see. Sorry."

"No prob. They're a little stale, I'm afraid."

Martin carefully unwrapped a single taffy, slipped the paper into his vest pocket, then sucked on the candy, lapsing back into another apparent coma.

Like all prep schools, Braddington was home to the dysfunctional castoffs of many rich, broken homes. Everyone's parents were divorced, everyone was crazy. There was Waldo Aronson, for example, whose great-grandfather had invented the gas pump, and who was said to be one of the two or three wealthiest kids in the entire world. Waldo never went anywhere without this big fat black leather briefcase and he had this ridiculous laugh that was more of a bark.

Or there was Myra Carmody, whose father published the phone book. Myra was a multimultimillionaire. But she was so cheap that she always dressed in clothes from the local thrift shop.

But even among a highly eccentric student body, Martin Rucker stood out. For one thing, he almost never showered. And—no big surprise—he usually smelled cheesy and rank.

"So . . ." Jack said as gently as he could, "I haven't

seen you around much lately, neighbor. Where have you been hiding?"

As if he didn't know.

Martin's room, 3-H, was a tiny single, which he kept in the style of a garbage dump. Simmons had long ago given up trying to get the boy to clean it up. Everything Martin owned was piled in the center of the floor, as if Martin were preparing a giant bonfire. More junk covered his bed, so he usually slept—when he did sleep—on his dirt-encrusted Oriental rug. Martin owned several original Chagalls and other incredibly valuable paintings, and sometimes when he took a nap he piled them on top of himself like blankets, because he said it made him feel safer.

As disgusting as his room was, the poor guy practically lived in there, except for classes. Rucker had gotten in trouble more than once for hoarding food from the cafeteria, trying to fill his big thermos from the milk machine so he could skip meals and come out of his cave less often.

"Where have I been, Jack?" Martin looked around the room, as if the answer might be in one of Jack's possessions. "Oh," he said distractedly, "I've been around, Jack, I've been around. You know me."

Martin rubbed his face, which was toad-belly pale and not just a little green. Students at Braddington were required to be in bed with lights out by ten-thirty. Eleven for seniors. But it was well-known that Rucker periodically went on no-sleep jags and stayed up three or four nights in a row, guzzling coffee that he made on an illegal hot plate. If you listened at Martin Rucker's door really late, you could almost always hear the clickety-clack of Martin typing on his computer. Or you'd hear the soft sounds of his favorite record playing over and over. It was a children's record. *Uncle Phil Sings Your Favorite Nursery Rhymes.* Some cheery-voiced guy singing "Little Jack Horner," that kind of thing. Rucker sang along, in a crazy high-pitched voice.

When Martin was walking around the campus with his strange bouncing gait, he often sang the songs to himself. He started singing one now.

"Jack and Jill went up the hill, to fetch a pail of waterrrrr. . . ."

Jack started.

"Jack fell down and broke his crown," Martin sang on, tapping his leg in time to the song.

Jack grinned. "Why are you singing that?"

"And Jill came tumbling afterrrr. . . ."

"Martin. Hold up. Why are you singing that?"

Martin looked at him with blank surprise. "What do you mean? You know I love those songs, Jack. And that one's got your name in it. Ha-ha."

"Uh-huh. Is that all?"

Martin tilted his head, as if puzzled. "What else could there be? Ohhhhh, I know. It's got your *girl-friend's* name in it too, right? Jack and Jill. That's soo funny!"

Martin had a long thin face that reminded Jack a little of Mr. Peanut on a Planter's Peanut Bar. Usually his face was either expressionless or frightened. But right now Martin did something Jack had never seen him do before. He grinned—a huge smile that seemed to split his face wide open.

It was frightening.

"Then up Jack got and off did trot," sang Martin, trotting his fingers back and forth across the chair, "as fast as he could caperrr. . . ."

"Okay, Martin, that's enough."

Martin made a baby face. "You don't like my singing?" He laughed, briefly, then frowned.

16

"No, it's not that," Jack said uneasily. A trickle of sweat ran down the base of his spine.

C'mon, he told himself. He'd be crazy to let a nutcase like Martin freak him out. But there was an image that had just popped up in his brain, like internal E-mail. And it wouldn't leave.

When he and Jill were sneaking into the room this afternoon, Jack had glanced at Martin's dark door. The peephole had been dark. Because the lights were off, Jack had assumed. But what if—

Martin was humming.

"Well!" Jack slapped his knees. "I guess I better get to work. I can't stay up late tonight studying, you know, 'cause we've got the meet against Andover, Friday." He ran his fingers through his auburn hair, letting the locks fall back in place.

"Yes, you better get to sleep early," Martin said. "I mean, I imagine you're rather tuckered out, shall we say." There was a twinkle in his pinkish eyes. "After the workout you got today."

Jack stared at him.

"Workout? What workout?"

Martin held both palms up and giggled like a little kid. "You tell me!"

Jack eyed him closely. But he couldn't read that crazy blank face.

"Did you have a good afternoon?" Martin asked.

Jack froze. "What are you talking about?"

Martin studied his nails girlishly.

"Martin? Did you hear what I said?"

"Uh-huh." Martin poked a grimy finger into his mouth, feeling around as he apparently tried to dislodge a stuck food bit. When he was done, he smiled happily. "Oh, by the way, I saw you," he said.

CHAPTER 3

IT WAS AS IF SOMEONE HAD TURNED ON A shower of ice water over Jack's head. He clenched his jaw so hard his teeth ground.

"You saw me?" he echoed, trying to make the statement sound absurd. "Saw me what?"

"Saw you with Jill. I saw you come in. And I saw you leave. I saw you."

"I don't know what you're talking about."

"Jack and Jill went up the hillll. . . ."

"Don't sing that anymore, Martin, I'm serious."

Okay, so he saw me, Jack was thinking, trying to stay calm. He still had nothing to worry about. Nothing. Nothing . . .

Martin crossed and uncrossed his legs. He looked at the ground and spoke even more softly and almost sadly. "You're mad at me, aren't you?"

The question took Jack by surprise, but in a way, it pleased him, too. So that's what this was all about. Crazy kid. It was just an excuse to get Jack to talk to him. He felt the old guilt rumbling. "Mad at you? Don't be absurd. Mad at you for what?"

"Yes, you are. You're mad at me. You don't like

me. Nobody likes me. I know." He laughed, but his eyes were filled with tears. "God has blessed me with keen powers of perceptiveness, you see, thus allowing me to notice that I am what is known as persona non grata, pariah to the world."

"Martin," Jack said. "First of all, you're exaggerating. Second of all, you don't let anybody know you. I've told you before. What do you expect if you hide? You expect to make a whole mess of friends when you're alone in your room?"

Martin didn't answer. "Are you my friend?" he asked.

"Of course I'm your friend."

"Then why did you say I had to leave before?"

More than anything else in the world at that moment, Jack wanted Martin out of his room. But what he said was, "I never said that. I mean, I know I said I had to study, but—"

"No, you're right," Martin said with a sigh. He stood up. "I should let you have your privacy."

Jack had to contain a sigh of relief. He was leaving. It was over.

"Besides," Martin said, "I should go down and see Simmons."

"See Simmons? About what?"

"Oh, this and that. You know. He's always saying we should tell him if we see students breaking rules. You know, for their own good. Isn't that part of the Braddington Code of Honor?"

Martin was studying the floor. Jack's first impulse was to pummel him. He had to scream at himself to settle down.

"You wouldn't do that," Jack said quietly.

"Oh, yes I would."

Jack tried to breathe deeply. Because right in the middle of his fury, he was thinking that Rucker was probably the most pathetic kid he'd ever known. If he relaxed and treated him nicely, he told himself, he could easily take care of this problem.

"Martin," he said, trying to get the anger out of his voice.

"Yes, Jack."

"Whatever you saw or think you saw this afternoon? Just forget about it. I mean, don't flip out, okay?"

"I'm not sure I follow you, Jack."

"Look. I happen to know that you stay up till all hours. I don't tell on *you,* right? We're on the same side, guy. It's us against them. I mean, what's your problem? You're suddenly some big stickler for the rules?"

"Oh, no," Martin said, waving his hand in the air. "Nothing like that. I don't care about the rules."

"Good."

"So," Martin said, scratching his ear. "I better be going."

"Going?"

"To see Simmons."

Jack felt another wave of nausea.

"Unless, of course," Martin said casually, "you really do want me to stay."

So that was it. "Of course I do!" Jack blurted out.

"But you said you had to study. . . ."

Jack forced a sickly grin. "Why don't we study together?"

"Oh, you don't really want to."

The sweat was coming more freely now. "Sure I do."

"It doesn't sound like you really mean it."

Jack paused. Martin was staring down at one of his scuffed black wing tips, studying the shoe with intense interest.

"I really want you to stay," Jack said.

Martin smiled up at him hopefully. "Really really?"

"Really," Jack said, almost gagging on the word.

Martin clapped his hands. "Oh, Jack," he said. He looked like he was going to cry. "I'm getting happy for once!"

Jack eyed him suspiciously. "You are?"

"I am, Jack. For the first time I see how a place like Braddington could be fun, know what I mean? Oh, of course you do, Jack, I mean, you—you're happy all the time. But for me, Jack. Oh, dear, Jack. I don't need to tell you, you know. For me life is just a constant misery. At least it was. Until now."

"Until now?"

"Uh-huh."

"Well, that's good, Martin. I mean, I'm glad to hear that. But I gotta admit, I'm a little curious. What's the change, if you don't mind my asking?"

"What's the change?" Martin echoed, blinking.

"Yeah. I mean, why are you suddenly so excited? Braddington is still the same trash hole it always was, right?"

"Well sure," Martin said. "But from now on, Jack old boy, we're going to be the closest of friends."

CHAPTER 4

JILL WAS SINGING. SWINGING HER ARMS, TOO. Then she saw the expressions on the faces of the students she was passing on the paths. The smiles. She covered her mouth.

But she couldn't help it. She felt so excited she wanted to throw back her head and howl like a wolf. She hadn't read a word this afternoon. The notebooks in her backpack didn't contain a single new note. She had wasted two hours in the library just staring into space.

The school bell struck six. She had reached the south end of campus. Practically skipping, she walked through the large iron gates with the big *B* for Braddington scripted in a steel circle up near the top.

According to Jack, most Braddington kids thought of the campus as a prison, and envied day students who could come and go pretty much as they pleased.

Some prison, thought Jill, with a laugh. At Braddington, almost all of the "inmates" were fabulously rich. These kids were on their way to the finest colleges and the brightest futures America had to offer.

The real prison was the town. Down the hill, where Jill was now headed. Braddington, New Hampshire—a grimy little pit if ever there was one. With every block Jill passed, the houses became smaller and more run-down.

When she was at school, Jill felt free. Whenever she was in town, she could feel the place sinking its hooks back into her.

Well, not today. Today she had a magic shield. And scrawled across that shield in big bold letters was a name.

Jack.

As happy as she was, Jill kept her head down as she walked. It was an old habit. No matter what street she walked on in Braddington, if she looked up she could see the black smokestacks of the paper mill looming up over the housetops like evil sentries. And she hated looking at that.

Every morning, when Jill woke up in her second-floor bedroom in her tiny ramshackle house, she could see those same smokestacks belching black smoke. And just in case she ever managed to forget the place, the mill's whistle blasted long and loud every morning and every afternoon.

The mill. It was an ugly dark monster of a building that hulked along the almost equally ugly Passonic River. The river had once been pretty, but that was before the mill began dumping sewage in it. For sixty years they had been polluting it so badly that now only the dumbest white-trash kids in Braddington ever swam in it.

The mill. It *was* a monster—one that chewed up your loved ones and stole their lives. Jill's dad had worked there forever. So had her mom, until an accident at one of the pulp-pressing machines had cost her the use of her left arm. Jill had two older brothers,

James and Walter; both worked at the mill. And thanks to the constant roar of the machines, they were all hard of hearing. Except Walter. He hadn't been at the mill long enough. But Walter's hearing would go eventually, Jill knew; just like the rest.

She had reached the center of town, a small traffic circle with the dreary gray statue of Nathaniel Braddington standing guard in the middle. The guy looked about as miserable as most people in the town. Tightening her coat against the cold, Jill headed through the alley past the fire station. Almost home.

She'd always figured she'd work at the mill herself someday. No matter what her mom said. From the time Jill was a small child, her mom had given her a little lecture every night when she put her to bed. "You're different, Jill. And don't you ever forget it. You're smarter than the rest of us. If I hadn't been there, I'd doubt you were my own."

Jill didn't believe her. She was first in her class at the local high school and was bumped ahead two years—but it meant nothing to her. It wasn't a real test, she told herself. All her life she'd seen the boys and girls of Braddington Academy, strolling through her town, eating at Chez Henri, the expensive restaurant. The boys always wore jackets and ties and the girls dressed to kill in their fashionable clothes. The way they talked—you didn't even have to hear what they were saying. You could just tell these kids were Smart with a capital S. Jill could never compete with *that*, she was sure of it.

So sure that she had refused to apply to Braddington. But her mother wouldn't take no for an answer. One sunny Tuesday she had kept Jill home from school and marched her through the town, up the hill, and through those iron gates. Mrs. Marshack marched her right into the fancy glass building with the black-and-white sign that said ADMISSIONS.

"I'll be making some *admissions*," Jill told her mother as she stepped inside. "I'll have to *admit* that I'm really stupid."

But instead she had to fill out an endless application and then chat with a shiny, bald-headed man named James Bussman, who wore a vest and a red bow tie and laughed in a high-pitched voice at every other thing Jill said. Laughing *with* her or *at* her? Jill couldn't be sure.

Then she had to take an hour-long test.

One week later the call came.

When Jill's mom hung up the phone, she was crying, something her mother almost never did. Jill's first thought was that someone had died. Then she realized it was the school; she'd been turned down, as she knew she would right from the—

"You're in, Jill," her mom said.

Jill's jaw dropped. Her mother grinned through her tears.

That first year the pressure on Jill had been so intense she had barely been able to sleep at night. By the end of first semester she had given herself a bleeding ulcer and had to spend a week in the Braddington Infirmary under the supervision of mean Mrs. Mack, the head nurse. But Jill had gotten straight As. No mean feat at a school like Braddington, where half the kids were geniuses and all the teachers had Ph.D.s and assigned more homework than many colleges.

Slowly, Jill became more confident, more sure of herself. She began to realize she was smart after all. Smart with a capital *S* and maybe all the other letters as well. But the pressure was still there—always there, like a big rock strapped onto her back. Her mom, her dad, her brothers—they all expected so much from her. They were counting on her. To get out of the mill, the town. To become the first Marshack to go to college. To get rich.

She turned down Ivy Lane. Her oldest brother, James, had shoveled the sidewalk clean, but she tromped across the snow-covered postage-stamp of a lawn. She was only halfway to the house when she heard the phone.

"Phone!" she shouted as she slammed the front door shut behind her. Her mom's hearing was so bad, phone calls to the Marshacks often went unanswered.

Jill raced into the kitchen and grabbed the red receiver that hung by the battered swinging door. "Hello?"

It wasn't that she was too late. She could tell there was still someone on the line.

"Hello. Hello!"

The only answer was a tiny, sinister click.

And then a dial tone droned flatly in her ear.

CHAPTER 5

THAT NIGHT, JACK SLEPT POORLY. HE KEPT thinking there was someone in the room. But in the morning, when he woke up, he had a smile on his face and the warm wonderful feeling that everything was totally right with the world.

It was only when he opened his eyes that he remembered Martin.

Last night, Rucker had stayed in his room for hours, talking a mile a minute. He told Jack all about his childhood, getting dragged by his dad from country to country, how he thought he would like college more than he had liked prep school, why he wanted to go to Harvard (his father had gone there and his grandfather and his great-great-grandfather). He talked about how he wanted to write wonderful children's books someday. He said his books would be so kind and wise that they would keep future children from growing up lonely the way he had. And on and on and on and on . . .

At least, Martin didn't bring up Jill again. But he wouldn't take any kind of hint about Jack wanting to go to sleep, either. Finally Jack got into bed, turning out all the lights except his bed lamp. And still Martin stayed in his chair, talking talking talking in that soft lilting stream, like a crazy never-ending lullaby—

He just couldn't sleep anymore. He thought he and Jack really could be good friends and he was sorry if he was rude earlier. He hoped Jack didn't think he was threatening him in any way. He wished so much that he had a girlfriend of his own.

Jack fell asleep while Martin was talking. And when he opened his eyes sometime later, the bedside clock glowed 3:13. Martin was finally gone.

For the first time in a long time Jack considered locking his door. No way, he'd finally decided. It would only make things worse.

Besides, Martin had just been carried away. He wanted to feel powerful for once, Jack decided. He'd have to be careful with him. Handle him gently. But other than that . . .

That morning, when Jack was getting dressed for breakfast, the door to 3-H was closed and dark as usual. Jack kept his own door open while he picked out a school tie (red-and-black stripes with the coat-of-arms insignia) and a blue single-breasted blazer. Martin's door was still closed when Jack headed downstairs.

Braddington had a campus larger than some small colleges. There were two large cafeterias, one old (Buford) and one new (Carmichael). Basically, you were supposed to eat in the dining hall closest to your own dorm, but you were allowed to go to either. Whitmanites all went to Carmichael, a bright brick building. Inside were lots of polished gleaming brass and vast high windows. Long walnut tables varnished to a high gloss filled the dining hall. The cafeteria workers were all townies. As you pushed your tray down the line you could see the hate in their eyes as they ladled out the food to the rich kids. It was a lovely way to start the day.

And ever since the fall, those townie workers had made Jack think about Jill. If it wasn't for her scholarship, she could have ended up in a dead-end job like this one. That was one of the things that had made Martin's visit last night so terrifying. By sneaking her into his room, Jack had jeopardized Jill's entire future. He cursed at his own selfishness, his stupidity. If they were caught—

Well, that wasn't going to happen, he told himself. Only Martin had seen them.

He could handle Martin.

"Morning," Jack told the gray-faced woman in the white uniform who stood behind the chafing dishes holding a slotted metal spoon.

The worker didn't respond.

Though he wasn't feeling particularly hungry, Jack took his usual—scrambled eggs, three strips of well-grilled bacon, orange juice, and a cup of coffee. He glanced toward the varsity wrestling table. Naturally, it was the best table in the whole place, the center table, right in the sun.

Sitting at the middle of the table, a couple of textbooks open beside him, was a huge guy with short brown hair. One side of his jacket collar was turned up. His face looked puffy with sleep. On his plate sat a big steaming pile of flapjacks and sausages.

Jack smiled. Bradford.

Bradford Knox was a fellow Whitmanite, and the fourth member of their dorm's quartet of varsity wrestlers. For obvious reasons, Bradford wrestled in the unlimited weight class.

"Hey," Jack said, putting his tray down across from him.

"Hey," Bradford rumbled back. Bradford had a deep bass voice and the face of a bulldog.

"You ready for that chem test?" Jack asked him.

"I'm ready to flunk it."

"Excellent."

"You know what day it is today, Jack?"

"Uh, let's see, it wouldn't be Tuesday, by any chance?"

"That's right, Jack. Only two shopping days left before we bust those Andover wussies."

The meet was Friday. Andover was their arch rival. And it would be the third match between Jack and his own personal nemesis, Billy Dennehy. Dennehy had beaten Jack the first time they wrestled, two years ago. In fact, Dennehy was the only guy Jack had ever lost to. It didn't feel good, Jack noticed. The night he had lost, he had made a silent promise to himself; he would never lose again, and he had trained fanatically to make sure he'd won every match since.

Last year Jack had gotten his revenge on Dennehy, outpointing him in a seesaw battle that had come down to the last seconds. This Friday he intended to finish the job and pin Dennehy once and for all.

"We're going to cream them," Jack said.

Bradford agreed. "I hear you broke training yesterday," he added, with a little smile.

Jack looked at him sharply.

"Cameron told me," Bradford explained.

"Great!"

"What's the matter?"

Jack glanced around. No one was sitting at the nearest table, and no one was paying attention. He lowered his voice anyway. "He wasn't supposed to tell anyone."

"I'm not anyone."

"I know that, Bradford, but—"

"Hey, Jack, don't get all paranoid on me, wouldya? We're on the same team, remember?"

"That's not the point. I trust you with my life." This

30

was true, actually. "Ah, look, just don't tell anyone else, okay?" Jack poked at his globby eggs with a fork, but didn't take a bite. He couldn't believe Cameron had done that. Who else had he told?

"What's with you?" Bradford asked. "You seem so wired. You're supposed to be relaxed after an afternoon like that."

"Yeah," Jack agreed tensely.

"Let me ask you something. Jill's a day student, right?"

"Right."

"It's none of my business, but why didn't you go to her house? I mean, that's what I would have done, if I was an incredibly lucky guy such as yourself."

"Her house is out," Jack said. "Her mom's there all day, and Jill says she's stricter than faculty."

"Jack," Bradford said. "Would you lighten up? You're golden. Nobody saw you. Just don't do it again, would be my advice."

"Believe me, I won't."

"I mean, getting kicked out twice is a great honor, but three times . . . that's a little silly already, am I right?"

Bradford was smiling. Jack smiled back. The truth was, the big guy always calmed him down. Jack had often joked to Bradford that he should be a bodyguard when he grew up. He had that calm, fearless quality.

"Yeah," Jack said. "Three times would definitely not be the charm."

The first time Jack had been kicked out of Braddington was for getting into a fight with a senior, Hall Hunsinger, who kept ragging on him and short-sheeting his bed, stuff like that. Hall was older and a lot bigger, but Jack got so mad he won the fight easily. Unfortunately, Hall ended up with a major concussion. And Jack ended up hanging out at his father's

31

house in Groton, Connecticut, for an entire semester. That had truly seemed like a punishment worse than hell, and Jack had vowed never to get in trouble again.

The second time he got kicked out was for streaking stark naked (except for red high-tops and a ski mask) through a faculty meeting. They'd been meeting to discuss kicking out a friend of Jack's, and he'd felt compelled to express his support.

How he got caught for that one, he never knew. But after the second expulsion, Jack's father had added a special clause to his million-dollar trust fund. If Jack got into any more serious trouble, either with the school or with the law, before he turned twenty-one, his trust fund reverted to dear old dad. Jack's loving stepmother, Gilda, had convinced Mr. Washburn to add this delightful little codicil to the trust. Jack had been toeing the line very carefully ever since.

Until yesterday.

"Bradford, do me a big favor, wouldya? Tell me everything's going to be all right."

"Everything's going to be all right."

"Thank you. I feel so much better now."

"I mean it, man. You're fine. What are you worrying about?"

"I just can't believe I did it. I'm serious. I mean, that was like the stupidest thing I've ever done in my life. And I've done some stupid things, as you know."

"Likewise, I'm sure."

Jack grinned. One Saturday night, Bradford had gotten particularly frustrated that his heartthrob, Dede Connell, wouldn't go out with him. To ease the pain, he had gotten totally blitzed. That night (he claimed it was in his sleep) he pissed on his radiator. Bradford hadn't been nailed for the drinking, but there was no hiding the smell of hot urine, which stunk up the entire building. Bradford was put on dorm restrictions (in by seven, lights out by ten) for a whole month.

Jack tossed down his fork in disgust. "What was I thinking of, pulling a stunt like that!"

"I know *exactly* what you were thinking of," said Bradford through a mouth full of pancakes.

"Gentlemen," said a voice behind Jack.

A tall thin senior with shoulder-length dark hair that made him look sort of like a preppy musketeer dropped his tray with a bang next to Jack's.

"The Huntster," Bradford said.

"Day two hundred and thirty-one of the hostage crisis," Hunt said sourly. "God, I hate this place."

Out of the four Whitman wrestlers, Hunt Lowry was probably the most talented athlete, though he was erratic and moody. He was also, if you went by what girls said, the best-looking guy among Jack's circle. With his dark eyes and sharp thin features, Hunt certainly had quite the reputation for using girl after girl, and being utterly bored by his own prowess.

Hunt slapped Jack on the back. "Heard about yesterday." He whistled. "Nice going, Captain."

"What is this?" Jack asked, feeling a fresh stab of panic. "The whole school knows?"

"Yeah, and you should hear what the faculty is saying." Hunt scraped his chair back, sat.

"Very funny. Seriously. How'd you hear?"

"I forced it out of Cameron. Jack, remind me to give my French notes to Dede, would ya?"

Bradford's head jerked up.

"Bradford, would you stop acting surprised every time I drop Dede's name?" Hunt said. "It's getting on my nerves."

Bradford chewed a mouthful of pancake and eyed Hunt silently.

33

"He's trying to make me feel guilty," Hunt told Jack.

"No, he's not," said Jack.

"He is. Look at him. It's not going to work, Bradford. My parents have already filled up my guilt quotient. There's no room at the inn."

Hunt had been seeing Dede for two weeks now, which made things a little tense among the gang, since Bradford had been pursuing her for a year. Jack wished there was something he could do to protect Bradford's feelings, but what? The poor guy was all heart, like a huge Saint Bernard.

"What do you want me to say?" Hunt demanded. "She's a beautiful girl and she French-kisses like a wildcat. There, are you satisfied?"

"Hunt," Jack said. "Cut it out."

"Look at him—he's driving me crazy."

"He's not saying a word."

"He's saying it with his eyes."

Bradford smiled. "I'll say this, Hunt. Don't hurt her, you understand?"

"Oh, now what is that? Is that blatant or what?" Hunt said. "Look at this. He thinks he's her father or something."

"Don't hurt her," Bradford repeated. "Case closed."

When Bradford said case closed, people listened. Even Hunt shut up.

"I'll say this," Hunt said finally. "I'd hate to be Bradford's opponent on Friday."

"That's the truth," Bradford agreed with a big grin. He and Hunt banged forearms, first left, then right, then did the team whoop, starting soft and getting louder and louder. Several students around the dining hall gave a cheer. Wrestling—and beating Andover— were among the school's top priorities.

Jack grinned with relief as Bradford and Hunt sat back down. So what if Bradford and Hunt both knew about him and Jill? These guys were his closest friends. But nobody else could ever find out—ever.

"There's the little devil," said Dede Connell, joining their table. " 'Casanova' Washburn the Third." The thin pretty blond girl sat next to Bradford and across from Hunt—but she was smiling at Jack. She was smiling warmly, but still—

Jack felt the wave of tension return.

With her short-cropped hair and pert features, Dede had the kind of classy good looks that you could just tell came from money. Jack couldn't remember, if he ever knew, how her family came by its wealth, but her dad owned some famous race-horses, he knew that. Dede herself kind of reminded Jack of a prize filly, the way she had such great carriage and poise.

Jack had his head in his hands.

"What's wrong?" he heard Dede ask. "Did I say something wrong?"

"He only wanted half the students to know," Hunt explained.

"How did you hear?" Jack snapped.

"Oh, I'm sorry, I didn't know it was a secret, I—"

Dede had these big amber doe eyes. She was a soft touch, and those eyes welled up easily. Like now.

"Dede, it's okay," Jack said. "I didn't mean to bark at you. It's just—I want to know how you found out."

"Brooke told me. But don't worry," she said sincerely, "I won't tell a soul."

"It's being written up in this week's *Braddingtonian*," cracked Hunt. "Once the paper comes out, you can tell whoever you like."

So far Hunt hadn't really greeted his new girl-friend. She was looking at him, obviously waiting for some kind of hello. "Hey," she told Hunt with a little smile. He nodded back, only barely acknowledging her presence.

It's starting already, Jack thought.

Hunt never broke up with his women, he just treated them so badly that they eventually gave up.

"Look at you," Bradford told Dede. "Three pieces of toast with no butter. No wonder you're such a stick. How can you live on that?"

"I don't like breakfast," Dede said.

"She doesn't like breakfast," Bradford said to Jack. "Did you ever hear of something like that?"

"It's a girl thing," Jack said.

"What's a girl thing?" asked Brooke as she and Cameron brought their trays over to join the crowd.

"Not eating," explained Hunt. His eyes sparkling, he gave Brooke that sexy grin of his. Jack caught him doing it, then cut a glance at Dede; she had seen it, too, because her face had fallen. More trouble in paradise.

Brooke, who had a big mass of red curls, never wore her hair the same way twice. Today she had piled her hair up high on her head like a headdress. She was wearing lip gloss, too, which made her cupid's-bow lips look even more kissable than usual.

"That's not a girl thing, Jack," Brooke said in a husky voice. "I'm hungry all the time."

She started massaging Jack's shoulders.

"Brooke, c'mon," Cameron told her, nudging her to sit down.

"What's your rush?"

"We've got about ten minutes left before they close the place."

"So?"

Cameron was giving her a stern look.

"What?" Brooke asked, feigning surprise.

Brooke was into acting, and had starred in a couple of Dramat all-school productions. Jack happened to think she was an excellent actress—onstage. Offstage she always seemed like she was imitating a real live person, rather than just being one.

"Soooooooooooooo?" Brooke asked Jack, when she and Cam had sat down. "How did it go?"

"Yeah," Hunt said. "We want a few details. Is it true what they say? Are townie girls more fun?"

Jack shot a finger into Hunt's face. "Watch it," he said.

"Whooo," said Hunt, faking fear. "Sensitive."

"Guys," Cameron said, not looking around, just sipping his coffee. "Can I make a suggestion here? We table this discussion right now. And that includes any and all references to what happened yesterday. I'm talking today, tomorrow, and from now and for all time unto eternity. We did it, we got away with it, cool. But if that rumor ever spreads? It could get very hot for us, understood?"

Hot for *us*, thought Jack. That was nice of Cam to say. Because as Cam well knew, if the heat ever came down for yesterday's break-in, Cameron would only catch it for taking the key—probation probably. *Us.* Right then, Jack forgave Cameron for telling Bradford.

"Cameron's right," Dede said tensely. "We shouldn't talk about this."

There was an awkward silence.

"So what are we supposed to do?" Brooke asked loudly. "Just sit here without saying anything just because Jill snuck into Jack's room?"

She guffawed. Cameron jabbed her hard in the ribs. Now she squealed. "Ow! What's the matter with you?"

"What's the matter with *you*?" Cameron asked

back. He said it quietly but with such intensity that Brooke shut up. "I mean, are you insane?"

"Look," Brooke said, "let me let you all in on a little secret. If you want to hide something, you don't act suspicious. You just act natural. Then no one suspects a thing."

"Just drop the subject," Cameron said. "Permanently. It's that simple."

Brooke shrugged. "Okay. Be humorless."

Cameron turned away from her. He pushed his frameless glasses up the bridge of his nose. "There's a motion on the table. Let's call it the we-don't-bring-it-up rule."

"I second the motion," Dede said.

"Good," said Cameron. "Everyone agreed?"

Everyone voted by their silence.

"Good. Then we're all clear?" Cameron asked the table.

Everyone nodded.

I am such an idiot, Jack was thinking. He felt so disgustingly helpless. He trusted his friends, but he and Jill had a secret now, a secret with so much riding on it. And it wasn't something they could just keep to themselves. People already knew. Martin, for instance. Suddenly it was like his life was in other people's hands.

It didn't make him feel any better when Hunt draped his arm around his shoulder and said, "Listen, Captain, can I hit you up for a ten spot? My lousy parents forgot to send me my allowance again."

Hunt had borrowed money from Jack before; he wasn't so great about paying it back either. That wasn't what Jack was thinking about. Why did Hunt ask *him*? And this morning of all times. Was it because he knew that Jack wouldn't dare to refuse *him*? Now that Hunt *knew* about yesterday?

38

"If it's a problem, don't sweat it, I'll just—"

"No, no. No problem." Jack pulled out his wallet. Bradford was right; he *was* getting paranoid. If Hunt *didn't* bum money off him, now that would have been something to worry about. He tossed a ten onto Hunt's tray. Then he glanced up at the big round wall clock.

Morning prayer was in exactly ten minutes. The cafeteria was filling up now with the last-minute rush—kids grabbing breakfast so they wouldn't be starving to death waiting for the cafeteria to open again for lunch. Jack was feeling like what he really needed was to get some air—and some privacy.

But over by the front doors, against the backdrop of multicolored overcoats that hung on the wooden pegs, Jack saw a familiar gray blur go loping by.

His eyes focused.

His heart sank.

Oh, no . . .

CHAPTER 6

"HEY," HUNT SAID. "LOOK WHO CRAWLED OUT from under his rock."

Everyone looked up as Martin Rucker bounced over to the food line with his crazy rolling gait.

"He must have run out of supplies," Brooke said. "Hey, Cam. Is it true about the rat?"

In one of the hundreds of stories that always swirled around kids as strange as Rucker, rumor had it that Martin had once kept an illegal pet rat in his room. According to the legend, the rat had died, but Rucker kept the dead carcass in his cage until other kids started noticing the odor and the flies.

"Nah," Cameron said. "That's all made up. He just smells bad 'cause he never washes."

"How about that business that he killed his brother and sister when he was six?" asked Hunt.

"Bull," Jack said tersely. "He's an only child."

"Sure," said Hunt. "*Now* he is."

"How do you know it's not true?" Brooke asked Jack.

"Because Jack's the big Rucker fan, aren't you?" teased Hunt.

"Get off."

"They're neighbors," Cameron explained.

"Jack used to be the only guy he'd talk to," Bradford said.

"Now he won't talk to anyone," said Dede.

Jack forced himself not to turn and look and see if Rucker was coming over to his table. As it turned out, he didn't need to look.

"Don't look now," Brooke said, "but I think the fungus is among us." She didn't say it that quietly, either.

"Jack?" It was Martin's strange whispery voice.

Jack felt his face flush. He pretended not to hear.

"Jack?"

He turned. "Yeah, hi, Martin, how are you?"

Martin beamed. "I'm rather superbly excellent, as a matter of fact, thank you for asking. Good morning to you all, by the way. Well, Jack. As you can see, I took your advice."

"Oh? What advice is that?" Jack asked.

"You told me to get out of my room so I'd make some new friends." He sat down next to Brooke, who made a little face for the benefit of her friends and moved her chair several inches away. Jack glared at her. Martin didn't smell *that* bad. That was all he needed, his friends snubbing Martin and making him madder and more jealous than he already was.

"Oh, Jack," Martin said, putting his hand over his heart. "I've got to tell you. Last night's talk really helped me. I don't know how to thank you."

Jack could feel everyone's eyes on him.

"I'm glad," he said.

"Thank you thank you thank you."

"Sure."

Martin kept beaming at him until Jack looked away.

41

"I don't know if we've ever been introduced," Martin said, holding out his grimy hand to Brooke. "I'm Martin Rucker."

"Hi," Brooke said, giving him a little smile but not taking his hand.

"Oh, goodness, I know this was—what? Two years ago? But I thought you were really splendid in *The Glass Menagerie* as that bossy mother."

"Typecasting," Cameron said. Brooke glared at him.

Hunt picked up his tray. "Well, I'm out of here. See you jerks later."

Jack could see the torn look on Dede's face. She didn't want to insult Martin by leaving the moment he sat down, but she wanted to be with Hunt. "You headed over to assembly?" she asked.

"Nah," Hunt said as he started bussing his tray. "I thought I'd go for a little moose hunt in Maine."

It's definitely starting, thought Jack.

And then they were gone.

"Well," Brooke said, making another big face at Jack. "I guesssss, Cam? We better hit the road, too, whaddaya say?" She was rolling her eyes and nodding her head in Martin's direction in the most obvious way possible. If Martin didn't catch what was going on, he was brain-dead.

Cam had his mouth full of blueberry muffin, but he turned and looked at the clock and then nodded. "Right," he said in a garbled voice.

And then Cam and Brooke were gone as well.

"So how you been doing, Rucker?" Bradford asked him. "It's nice to see you out of that goddamned room of yours for once, let me tell you."

Good old Bradford, thought Jack. The big guy would talk to anyone.

Martin blew his nose loudly into his soiled handkerchief. "Thank you, Bradford. It's very nice to be out. And like I say, I owe it all to Jack. But the good news is, I'm not going to make this a onetime thing. I'm really making a commitment to change. From now on, I'm going to have breakfast with you guys every morning. Right, Jack?"

Assembly hall at Braddington, where they held morning prayer at eight A.M. each and every week-day, was a huge rotunda. Seating was by age, with the first formers sitting all the way up in the balcony and the seniors down in front. Girls had their own special section off to the front left. Jack looked for Jill but didn't see her.

In each section seats were assigned alphabetically. Washburn and Rucker—the letters were far enough apart to put several rows of students in between them. That was a relief, because Martin had tailed along with Bradford and Jack all the way over here, provoking plenty of stares.

Jack glanced behind him. He caught a glimpse of Martin's head, bent as if in reverent attention to the speaker.

Morning prayer only lasted about ten minutes. It was mainly a way of making sure everyone was up before first period. This morning's speaker was Dean Schmidt, a bowling ball of a man who had been an All-American fullback for the Braddington Bears when he went here in the sixties. He stood gripping the podium, glaring out at them. Behind him hung the huge wooden model of Braddington's coat of arms.

"You are the future leaders of America," Dean Schmidt reminded them, as he did whenever he led morning prayer. "What do we ask of you? As Braddingtonians, in the great tradition of our school,

43

we ask, above all, honor. Courage. Valor. And hard work."

"We ask that you stay out of the girls' dorms," whispered Wallace Wasserman, the nerdy kid sitting to Jack's right. Jack's head jerked in his direction, startled. Wallace flinched. He was just joking, Jack realized. He smiled. Wallace smiled back with obvious relief.

"What is our ethic?" Dean Schmidt asked, booming into the microphone. He pounded the lectern. "If you learn nothing else in your years at Braddington, let it be this. You must keep your bottoms on the chair until the work is done! Let us pray."

Everyone bowed their heads. Jack resisted the impulse to look for Rucker again. He had the awful feeling he would see the wacko with his head lifted high, staring straight at him.

A minute later the bell rang for first period and the great sea of students started pouring out into the frigid morning air. Once outside, Jack flipped up the collar of his coat. Students were racing every which way along the Parcheesi-like grid of slate paths as they hurried to their first period classes. Just then, Jack felt Martin's soft touch on his arm.

He turned, angry. "Look, give me a—"

But it wasn't Martin standing there with that dopey innocent look of his; it was Jill, with those gorgeous green eyes, eyes that right now were filled with surprise. She gave a little smile. "Sorry," she said. "I didn't know you were off-limits."

"Jill!"

It had only been a day; it felt like a year. He gave her a hug, right then and there. She laughed, delighted.

Then he said, "C'mon," jerking his head. They started walking again. He set a fast pace, hoping to leave Martin far behind.

She hooked her arm through his. She was wearing that green bulky pea coat of hers. Jack adored that coat. Love was like that. Everything about the person started to seem so special. The coat was actually kind of ugly. To Jack, it seemed extraordinary. And right now Jill looked so fresh-faced and beautiful. She leaned over and kissed his cheek as they walked, their faces bumping.

"You rabbit," he said. He had given her the nickname because of the cute way she liked to wrinkle the tip of her nose when she wanted to express mild disapproval.

"Killer," she said. With his wavy brown hair and strong jaw, Jill had often told him that he was more handsome than any movie star she'd ever seen. She said that Jack had looks that could kill. Hence the nickname. "You sleep okay?" she asked.

"Yeah," he lied. "You?"

She nodded. Then she stopped, pulling on his arm so that he stopped, too. They were standing only yards away from where they had stood yesterday, when he had told her his whole idiotic scheme. Only now the quad was swarming with kids. Jill glanced around, making sure no one was listening. Jack glanced around, too, but for different reasons.

"Jack?"

"Yeah?"

"I gotta tell you. Yesterday afternoon? I loved every minute of it. But when I said I slept well last night? I lied. I had nightmares all night, Jack. I think that's the most scared I've ever been in my entire life."

"Don't worry," Jack said. "We won't repeat it."

"Oh." Her face fell.

"What's wrong?"

"That's what *I* was going to say," she said. "But I don't like hearing you say it. You're supposed to find me irresistible. You're supposed to beg me to sneak into your room every day."

"Jill, believe me, I would, but—"

He stepped closer. "We shouldn't talk about this here."

"I know, sorry." She bit her lip. "I was going to surprise you at breakfast but . . . I was kind of embarrassed."

"Embarrassed? Why?"

"I figured Brooke and Cameron would be there, looking at me funny. *Knowing.* You know."

Brooke and Cameron—they weren't the only ones who knew, thought Jack, heartsick.

"What?" she asked, reading his expression. *"What?"*

"Uh, actually . . . Hunt . . ."

"He knows, too?"

"Calm down—and don't talk so loud—yeah, and . . . and Bradford." Each name felt like he was giving her another knife twist.

Jill didn't answer. Her mouth was open.

"And Dede."

"Oh my God! You told me yesterday that we would keep this totally secret except for—"

"I know, I know, and it is. They're my best friends, Jill."

"Who told?"

"What's the difference?"

"What's the difference!"

"Cam told Bradford and Hunt. Brooke told Dede."

And Martin saw it all for himself, he thought. But he couldn't tell her that. Couldn't add that final nail to the coffin. Not now.

"Okay," she said, as if to herself. "Okay, okay." She looked up at him, smiling. "It's okay, right?"

"Yeah."

"You swear?"

"I swear."

Her smile broadened. "Sorry I got so snippy, it's just—"

She didn't have to finish the sentence. He knew what she meant. It was just that her entire life was on the line.

She squeezed his arm, gave him another quick peck, then turned right, toward her religious studies class with Reverend Morrissey. Jack knew Jill's entire schedule by heart. "Twelve-thirty, right?" she asked, walking backward.

They had made plans yesterday, before she left his room.

"Twelve-thirty," Jack called to Jill, smiling.

Jack stopped smiling as soon as she turned away.

"You know how Fowler is, right?" Jill asked.

"I ought to," said Jack. "I had him for physics. He threw me out of class twice."

"Okay. So you know how he announces the grades out loud as he hands back the papers?"

"Right."

"So he's going around the room, handing back the tests. B, C, D—"

"Was that Bradford?"

"What?"

"Was that Bradford who got the D?"

"Oh. No."

"Good. 'Cause this morning, he claimed he was going to flunk."

"I think he got a B-plus."

"Typical," said Jack. "I'm telling you, everybody thinks he's just a dumb jock. But Bradford is super smart. He's a computer whiz. Did I ever tell you that?"

"Yeah," Jill said. "Now let me finish."

"Sorry."

But before Jill could continue, she was interrupted again, this time by the tuxedoed waiter.

They were sitting, Jack and Jill, as close together as they could get in the second-to-last black leather banquette in the back of Chez Henri. Henri's was a small French restaurant with mahogany wainscoting and tangerine-colored tablecloths with cloth napkins to match. It was the last kind of place you'd expect to find in a town like Braddington, which featured such fine eating establishments as Joe's Diner and Greasy Betty's.

Henri was kept in business by the rich visiting parents of Braddingtonians, who always took their children out to eat in a belated attempt to get close to them. Since most of these parents were divorced, on parents' weekend it was not uncommon for students at Braddington to be taken out to Henri's twice in one day, first by one parent, then by the other. Henri was getting to be a rich man.

Townies, of course, couldn't even afford to eat the appetizers. And when Jill had confessed yesterday that she'd never set foot inside the place, Jack had invited her out to lunch on the spot.

"Do you want to hear ze specials?" asked the tall waiter. He had a thin black mustache and a slight, fake French accent.

Jack looked down at the two tall black leather menus fanned gracefully on the table in front of them—unopened. "I think we need another minute," he said.

The waiter frowned but left, moving on to whomever was sitting in the very last banquette.

"The waiter hates us," Jack said.

"Good," said Jill. "So where was I? Oh, yeah. So

48

then Fowler comes over to me— Jack, don't do *that*. We're in a restaurant." She giggled.

"I can't help it," he said. "I'm so in love with you I'm going out of my mind. I'm not kidding."

She kissed his cheek. "I don't have a problem with that."

"Anyway, finish your story," he said.

"It's a good thing you said that, or I would have been mad." He laughed.

"So when he gets to me, Fowler doesn't say a grade. He just says, 'Cheater.'"

"What?"

"Just like that. 'Cheater.' And drops my paper on my desk."

"He is such a—"

"Turns out," said Jill, "I got a perfect score."

"All right!" said Jack.

"So did Missy Handler, one seat away."

"Oh."

"Exactly. So now Fowler is accusing me of plagiarism."

"With what evidence? I mean, how come he doesn't think Missy copied off *you*?"

"'Cause Missy's a rich brat—present company excepted—and I'm a poor townie. And everyone knows, townies are either sluts or retards, depending on their gender."

"What a scumbucket Fowler is."

"So after class I go up to him."

"Good for you."

"I walk right up to him and I said, 'Mr. Fowler! How dare you accuse me of cheating?'"

"You said that?"

"'I have never broken a single Braddington rule in my life, Mr. Fowler!'"

"That, by the way, is no longer true," Jack pointed out.

"I know," Jill said. "Right after I said it I started picturing you and me yesterday and what we were doing and *where* we were doing it and my face turned like beet red. But I think he just thought I was angry, so it was okay. Anyway, he mumbled something mildly apologetic, something about leaving the whole thing up to me and my sense of honor. You know, the old Braddington Code of Honor. I'm supposed to turn myself in if I'm guilty and congratulate myself if I'm innocent."

"Congratulations," Jack said. He raised his water glass in a toast, clinked her glass, then kissed her. The feel of her soft lips against his sent a fireball through his body. It was like he disappeared for a second, leaving nothing but burning ash in his seat.

She started ripping pieces off her French roll, dabbing them into the pat of butter. Tell her about Martin, he ordered himself. Instead, he just sat there, smiling.

"This is probably not the way you're supposed to do this, right?" Jill asked, blushing. "You're supposed to use this little butter knife. C'mon, you can tell me. I've never been in a place like this before, I'm sure I'm breaking all the rules."

"You're doing great." *Tell her!* "Uh, Jill?"

She had her mouth full. "What?"

"There's something . . . I wanted to tell you."

She chewed, swallowed, waited. But when he didn't say anything more, she rushed on, lowering her voice. "Listen, I don't want to start whining or anything, but I am still a little nervous, in case you didn't notice. You know, about—"

"I know."

"But I figure it's like by tomorrow two whole days will have gone by with nothing happening, and then three, and then pretty soon we'll have forgotten all about it, right? Except I'll never forget about it, you know what I mean? Okay, now what did you want to tell me, Killer?"

How could he tell her now?

But he had to.

"Uh, it's just that . . . see—"

The waiter started toward their table again; Jack waved him off. The waiter was scowling openly now as he moved past him to the last banquette.

"What?" Jill asked, studying his face. "Oh God. Jack. No. You look so serious."

"No, don't worry, it's nothing major. It's just—"

"Just *what?* You're married. What am I saying? You're only eighteen. Aren't you? Wait a minute. You're actually, what? Thirty? And you've been kicked out of Braddington twenty times. Oh, I knew this was all too good to be true, I knew it. What? Tell me."

"No, no, no. It's just—last night, someone—"

"Jack!"

The voice was right above Jack's head, almost as if someone were talking inside his own brain. He turned.

Martin's head was right above his, grinning down like a gargoyle.

CHAPTER 7

THE SIGHT OF MARTIN STARTLED JACK SO
badly he knocked over his water glass. Jill jumped to
her feet, then started using the tablecloth to wipe up
the spill, which was dripping off the edge of the table
down into their laps.

Martin came around, standing in front of their
booth, giggling as he apologized. "I'm sorry, but the
look on your face, Jack—it was quite amusing."

Jack just stared at him. He felt reasonably confident
that the look on his face was no longer so amusing,
but Martin kept laughing in a forced, phony way.

"Well, no harm done, right?" said Martin. "It's just
water." He slid into the booth next to Jack. "Seems
like old times, eh, Jackie?"

"Martin," Jack said, ignoring the reference. The
anger was loud and clear in his voice. "If you don't
mind . . ."

Martin kept smiling. "I was sitting there hearing
these voices and I was thinking, that guy sounds so
familiar, but I couldn't tell who it was."

"You were eavesdropping," Jack said.

"Well, yes, I confess I was. And it was such a

52

charming conversation. Really, Jack, 'So in love that you're going out of your mind.' A bit clichéd, no? But sweet, sweet."

"I'm going to—"

"Going to what, Jack?"

Jack was going to say "kill you," but he swallowed the end of the threat. The words were so hard to get back down he actually gulped.

"Martin Rucker," Martin said, grinning his unbrushed teeth at Jill.

Jill gave a little smile back. "Jill," she said. "Uh, Marshack."

"You're a lucky girl, Jill," Martin lisped, nodding at Jack. He winked.

"Oh, I know."

"Very very lucky."

"Thank you. I feel the same way."

"I can't imagine there's a girl in the whole school who wouldn't want to—oh, dear, here I am chattering away and I haven't even asked if you two mind my joining you."

"Actually," Jack began.

"It's fine, of course," Jill said, giving Jack an odd look.

She thinks *I'm* being rude, thought Jack in amazement.

"Splendid. This is just the finest restaurant in town, don't you think?"

"By far," Jill agreed. "This is my first time."

"Your first time. How tender. I must kiss your hand." Martin reached across Jack.

"Martin, give me a break, would you?" Jack said, pushing him back in his seat.

"I'm sorry, Jack. It's just that I find true beauty so rare and . . . so dazzling."

"Hey," Jill said with a laugh. "I like that. Jack, where have you been hiding this guy?"

"You see, Jack," Martin said. "She likes me." To Jill he said, "I'll tell you a little secret about me. I'm actually a monster."

Jack was ready to agree to that.

Martin rushed on. "I'm kidding, of course. But I'll divulge a little bit of self-truth, if I may. You see, Jill, the fact is . . ." He leaned forward, his tie hanging down into the butter dish. "The thing is, I've lived my whole life trapped inside my head, you see. Always alone. So what did I do? I escaped into books. It was the only thing I could do. It was that or—"

He sat back, rubbed the tablecloth for a moment, looking as if he might cry. Then he looked up again, pasting the grin back on his face. "So, the result is, I only know what I've read. You—you must forgive me if I seem a little strange."

"You don't," Jill said. "Seem strange."

"That's a lie," Martin said. "I am strange. I know it. But I'm a real person, too. With real feelings. That's something a lot of people"—he glanced at Jack—"seem to forget."

Jack picked up his water glass. It was empty. He put it back down.

Martin told Jill, "Jack and I are neighbors, as I'm sure he's told you."

"Uh . . ." Jill gave Jack a questioning look.

"Oh, dear," Martin said, with a surprisingly charming smile. "He hasn't even mentioned me. Well, no matter. I'm sure he'll talk more about me in the future, right, Jack? I live right across the hall from Jack, you see. Three-H. But what am I saying? You couldn't possibly know what room I'm talking about. I mean, dear me, if you'd ever been inside Whitman Hall, you'd be thrown right out of the academy. Am I right?"

Jill hadn't gotten a perfect score on her chem test

by being slow. Jack wasn't sure just when she had caught on to the trouble, but she had definitely picked it up now. She glanced at Jack. He couldn't meet her eyes.

"Anyhoo," Martin said, clapping like a little boy, "I'm so excited to be eating here with both of you, I can't tell you. Yippee! Jill, by the way . . . the frog's legs at Chez Henri are the best I've had outside of Paris. Oh, waiter!"

He snapped his fingers high in the air.

Jill threw Jack a quick look, still smiling but making her eyes go all intense. It was a look that asked, "What is going on?" Jack tried to answer with a look that said he'd explain everything later.

The waiter arrived. "Monsieur," he said to Martin, "you are switching tables?"

"That is correct," Martin said. "I have run into some very dear old friends and they've asked me to join them."

Right, thought Jack. Like we had a choice.

"Very well," the waiter said, but he looked pretty angry. "I assume you are now ready to order?"

"You two haven't ordered?" Martin's eyes widened. "Oh, this is perfect! *Jack! Let me* order! Please? Let me! Let me! Just trust me, okay? I know all the best stuff. When I was six, I was ordering by myself in the world's finest restaurants."

Martin didn't wait for permission. He turned back to the waiter. "We'll start with a bottle of your finest wine." He saw the shocked look on the waiter's face. "Just kidding," he said. He turned back to Jill. "Though the truth is, in Paris, they gave me wine when I was four. But anyway—"

Opening the menu, Martin started rattling off a stream of perfect French. The waiter had to scribble rapidly to keep up.

55

"That is quite a bit of food, monsieur," the waiter said, when Martin finally finished.

"Yes?" Martin asked.

"For three people, I mean," said the waiter, with a worried look.

"Oh, I see," said Martin. "You're concerned about the expense?" He smiled as he patted Jack's shoulder. "Don't worry. This young man's a millionaire. Or he will be, if he plays his cards right. Right, Jack?"

The bill for the food Martin ordered came to a mere $249.67. When the check came, Martin started slapping the pockets of his musty suit. "My goodness, I don't have my wallet. How careless of me!"

He kept fumbling in his pockets until Jack took out his credit card. Martin thanked Jack profusely for picking up the tab. Then he ordered the waiter to wrap up the leftover food to go—and took it all himself.

And then—

He walked with them back to campus, chattering as happily as a bird, even skipping once or twice. There was no way to shake him, and no way for Jack to make a plan for meeting Jill later, without Martin hearing.

She looked terrified when they separated. The look on her face made Jack's heart ache.

After lunch on Tuesdays, Jack had American history with Mr. McNulty. So did Martin, who insisted on sitting next to him and passing him stupid notes such as, *Thank you again for lunch.*

Finally Jack wrote back, pressing down so hard on the paper that the pencil tore through in several places. *This has got to stop!*

Martin nodded thoughtfully as he read the note,

folded it, and slipped it into his pocket. Then he raised his hand.

"Yes?" Mr. McNulty called on him right away.

"Please you, kind sir. May I be excused?"

McNulty grimaced. Like most of the faculty, he hated Rucker. "What is it now?"

"I need to see Dean Schmidt."

"About what?"

"I can't say, sir."

"You can't say?"

"It's something very important, of that I assure you, but I need to speak about it to the dean directly."

Jack felt all the blood rush to his head and pound there so hard that he heard a strange clicking sound in his ears. He wondered if this is how it felt right before you had a stroke.

"The dean has regular office hours," Mr. McNulty said. "He's available to students almost every afternoon from three to five. Now sit down."

"But I need to see him now, sir. It's most pressing."

"You need to see him now?"

"Yes, sir, I do."

"No, you don't," Jack said quietly.

"What was that?" Martin asked him. "I'm sorry, Mr. McNulty, but my fellow classmate here was saying something to me and I didn't quite hear it. What was that, Jack?"

All eyes were on Jack now. He could feel the amazement, the shock, the ridicule, as his classmates caught on to the general idea of what was going down.

"I said, 'No, you don't,'" Jack said, slightly louder.

"No, you don't what?" Martin asked, giggling.

"Gentlemen," Mr. McNulty said, "if you two have some kind of drama to perform for us, I'd be delighted to schedule it into our syllabus. Provided, of course, that it has *something* to do with what we're talking about? Namely the Marshall plan!"

"Right," Martin said, sitting back down. "Sorry."

McNulty went on with his lecture. Jack kept his eyes focused on the teacher, but he could still see Martin, out of the corner of his eye, grinning wildly.

"Jill—Jill—*Jill!*"

Jack had to yell before the stream of questions and worries pouring out over the other end of the phone finally paused. "Jill, I'm telling you," he said. "There's not going to be a problem."

"How can you say that?"

"Because I'm going to talk to him, that's why."

"Talk to him?"

"Yeah. Talk to him. Tonight. As soon as we get off the phone."

"And say what?"

"Whatever. I'll find out what he wants."

"Oh, Jack, I'm so—"

"I'll find out what he wants, Jill, and whatever it is, I'll give it to him. I'll pay him if I have to."

"Pay him?! Jack! He's blackmailing you?"

"No, no, no. I just said that as an example. I mean, I don't know. The guy's such a head case, he probably doesn't even know what he wants. But whatever. I'll take care of it, okay?"

It was Tuesday night. Jack was in the common room, using the pay phone, which was the only phone in the dorm that was available to students. He kept turning around, double- and triple-checking that he was still alone.

"I'm so scared, Jack," Jill said.

"Well, don't be. That's ridiculous. There's absolutely nothing to be—"

"The way he kept singing those nursery rhymes all during lunch. Singing Jack and Jill, Jack and Jill . . . he seemed crazy, Jack."

"Oh, he's crazy, there's no doubt about that."

"So then—I mean—there's like no telling what he'll do."

Jack took a long deep sigh. He was so angry at Martin he wanted to rip the pay phone right off the wall. "Jill," he said, "all I can tell you is I'm going to take care of it."

There was a tense staticky silence at the other end of the line. "You're not going to hurt him, are you?" she asked.

"Jill, this is Jack. You know me. What do you think, I'm going to beat him up?"

The question hung in the air. He knew what Jill was thinking. Everyone knew about his famous fight with Hall Hunsinger.

"Will you call me back after you talk to him?"

"Yeah. How late can I call?"

Jill laughed bitterly. "You can call at three. It doesn't matter in this house. My parents are both hard of hearing, remember?"

"I'll call as soon as I can."

"Thanks. Oh, and Jack?"

"Yeah?"

"By the way, I still love you."

"I love you, too," Jack said. But it came out sounding more like a statement of anger than a term of endearment.

CHAPTER 8

JACK KNOCKED ON MARTIN'S DOOR. NO response. He knocked harder. Then he pounded. He thought about breaking the door down. It was after eight, which meant everyone had checked into the dorm already.

"I know you're in there, Martin," he said through the door.

Still no answer.

It was possible, he supposed, that Martin was in the bathroom or something. He decided to go back to his room and wait.

The wall switch in Jack's room was broken, which meant he had to cross to the desk to turn on the lamp, which meant that he didn't see Martin, just heard him softly singing.

"Jack and Jill went up the hill. . . ."

Jack flicked on the light.

Martin was lying on Jack's water bed, his socks resting on Jack's pillow. He had a big pile of books on the bed. He cackled. "Scared you, huh?"

"No, but I'm glad you're here, Martin. We have to talk."

"Goody."

Jack reached over and shoved the door so it slammed shut.

Martin sat up, swinging his legs off the side of the bed. "Jack and Jill went up the hillll . . . to fetch a pail of waterrrrrrrrrrrr. . . ."

"Shut up."

Martin made a face. "What's the matter, Jack? I thought you said you liked my singing."

"Well, I don't."

"Jackie, I'm surprised. You were always so kind to me in the past, I never thought you'd be the insulting type, like so many of our other fellow Braddingtonians." Martin laughed. Then coughed. He lolled his head from side to side like a baby. He yawned extravagantly.

"You followed me to lunch today," Jack said.

"So I did."

"You had no right to do that."

"But I did it anyway, didn't I?" Martin put his thumb on his nose and waggled his fingers. "And that's what you can do about it." He laughed himself into a wheezing fit.

"Martin," Jack said, and his voice was shaking. "If this is about when we were first formers, I—"

"Oh, it's not about that, Jack, it's not about that at all. I don't even remember that year." He wiped the air with his hand. "Pffft. Gone. That's the beauty of electroshock therapy. Reboots the whole system."

"Okay . . . then what do you want?"

"Want?"

"Yes, Martin. Why are you doing this? You want money? Is that it? You already sponged lunch off of me."

"Sponged lunch? Oh, Jack, I hope you don't think I forgot my wallet on purpose today. That old trick? Oh, no, no, no, I'm a very forgetful careless person.

61

You've seen my room, Jack. I'm not one of these hyperorganized types, as you know, and—"

"How much do you want? Here, let's figure the lunch at roughly two hundred bucks extra, including tax and tip. I'll bring that to an even five hundred, we forget the whole thing."

"But, Jack. I don't want money."

"You don't."

"No."

"Then what do you want?"

"Nothing."

"Martin, if you're trying to make me beat your face in, you're going about it the right way."

"But I don't want anything, Jack, I swear. You're already paying me, you see."

"I am?"

"Yes. Because I just want your friendship, is all. That's worth more to me than gold."

Jack felt a sudden need to sit down. He sat on the corner of his desk. He got up again almost instantly. He had a plan for what to say if Martin said something like this. It took him a moment to remember what it was, and a moment longer before he could manage to get the words out. He struggled desperately to put a nice face over his furious scowl. "We can't be friends, Martin. Okay? Not the way you want. You can see that, can't you? You and me, hanging out together, it's—"

Too late. Jack saw where this thought was going. Martin finished his sentence for him. "Ridiculous? For someone as handsome and popular as yourself to hang out with the grunge of the earth, namely me? Frankly, I agree. We're an odd couple. What can I say? I guess opposites attract."

"Martin, look. I like you. I do. You may not believe that, but I do. That's number one. But if you force

62

someone into hanging out with you, you can't expect them to enjoy that, can you? In fact, if you keep on forcing someone to do something they don't want to do, then they're going to start to hate you, right? Is that what you want? For me to hate you?"

Martin glowed like a lightbulb. "It's a risk I'll just have to take."

"Okay," Jack said, suddenly sawing the air with his hand. "That does it. I'll make this as plain as I can. You had your fun today. Good. Glad you got it out of your system. Because if you try anything like that ever again, I will tear you limb from limb. You understand me? They will find your guts strewn all over the quad, you got it, Rucker?"

"Guts all over the quad, yes, I think I follow that, Jack. It's a rather graphic image, so it's easy to grasp."

"I'm warning you!"

Martin crossed and uncrossed his legs and hunched over with his elbows on his knees. "Oh, now, I think that's enough of that, Jack. I mean, I really wouldn't threaten me, if I were you. In *fact*—"

The word spiked in volume. Martin gazed up at Jack. He was sitting up straight now. His eyes were dark, and the way his mouth was hanging open, it was almost as if his teeth had gotten sharper, as if he were growing fangs. "I'll do all the threatening from now on, if you don't mind," Martin said. "And here's threat number one." He cleared his throat. "Excuse me." He coughed into a fist. "Oh, dear," he said. He coughed several times more, this time using his soiled monogrammed handkerchief. "There. Now you see, Jackster, I've actually been rather nice to you today, letting you have a couple of slipups, as it were."

Martin's mouth worked, his jaw grinding as if he were chewing Jack into little pieces. "I let a lot of angry words go by, Jack. But from now on, here's how we'll play it. If you aren't very, very nice to me, I'll tell Simmons, and I'll tell Dean Schmidt—tell them exactly what you did."

Jack felt the top of his head blow off and splatter all over the parachute that billowed above their heads. His expression must have been frightening, because the dark look left Martin's face, his features softening back into their usual dull cast.

"Now you're obviously very angry with me, Jack. I can see that. Quite frankly, I'm not at all surprised that you want to beat my face in, as you say. I know you jocks go in for these barbarian expressions of your feelings. But I'm used to that, you see. My own dear gentle father is a great believer in corporal punishment. Something he picked up while in Asia, I believe. I daresay it was one of the only times we ever spent alone together, when it was time to give me six of the finest."

Martin swished a hand back and forth to demonstrate a cane lashing. "But," he said, "if you do beat me up"—another brief spasm of coughing—"I'll just go tell the dean anyway. Provided you don't succeed in killing me, ha-ha. In which case, of course, I'd get to rest for eternity and you'd go to jail. Food for thought, eh, Jackie? I mean, are you sure you want to get thrown out of school for a *third* time? What about that good-behavior clause in your trust fund and everything?"

This was one of the bad things about being popular. Everyone knew your stuff.

"You're right, Rucker. I'd be out a million dollars," Jack said. "Might be worth it."

Jack eyed Martin as coldly as he could. It was a look that he used before his wrestling matches to unnerve his opponents. But it didn't seem to be working on Rucker. He gave Jack a blank, questioning, almost cheerful look.

"Look, this is all ridiculous anyway," Jack said, trying to sound as confident as possible. "Go to Simmons, go to Schmidt, go to the moon for all I care. I mean you seriously think Simmons or Schmidt would believe you?" He forced a laugh. "You really think they'd take *your* word over mine?"

"Oh, yes, I do," Martin said. "Yes, I definitely do. I mean, it's not as if you've been such a perfect student up till now, Jack. All the guys adore you, to be sure, but the faculty? Besides, what possible motive would I have to accuse you falsely? Of course, if they have any doubts, I'm fully prepared to take a lie-detector test. How about you?"

Jack started toward him. Martin cringed. "Wait," he said quickly. "There's something else to consider. When I tell on you, I'll also tell on your friend Jill, uh, Marshack, is that it? So you'd be getting her booted as well, now wouldn't you?"

Jack's hands clenched into fists.

Martin made a face. "Nasty business. If I got a nice girl like that expelled, I'd be racked with guilt. She's on scholarship, isn't she? I doubt they'd even let her back in. It's only when you've got a father like yours who donates twenty big ones to the alumnae fund every year that they rush to readmit. So I—"

Jack lunged forward. Martin stood, scrambling backward, trying to get away as—Jack grabbed him by the lapels of his suit, pushing him back against the wall. He was about to snap Martin's head back when the look on Martin's face got through to him. Martin's eyes were shut, he was almost blissfully waiting for the blows to land. Jack let him go.

There was a knock on the open door and Cameron sauntered in. "Jack, I just got the munchies, big time; you want to order out for a pizza and some—" Cameron stopped short, obviously surprised to see Martin cowering by the wall. "Oh, hi, Rucker," he said. "Jack? Some 'za action?"

"Uh, no thanks."

"Come again?" Cameron said.

Jack was known for his love of junk food. He held the dorm record. Two whole pies in one night. "Uh, I'm not hungry," he said.

Cameron made a face, disappointed. "That's not like you, Jack, to turn down 'za."

Jack shrugged.

"Uh, Jack?"

Jack turned and stared at Martin as if he had forgotten the guy was still there.

"I think *I'd* like some pizza," Martin told him.

Jack just kept staring.

"Order me some 'za, Jack."

Jack felt his face flush, felt the tips of his ears burning. He looked at Cameron. He could see the shock on his friend's face. Cameron was obviously wondering why Jack didn't tear Martin's head off for talking to him that way.

"Uh, maybe . . . I'll . . ." Jack stammered. He couldn't get the words out. "Cameron, maybe I'll get some pizza after all," he finally said.

CHAPTER 9

ONE OF THE IDEAS THEY ALWAYS DRUMMED into you at Braddington was *Mens sana in corpore sano*, a healthy mind in a sound body. But when Jack woke up Wednesday morning, he felt like he had an insane mind in a body that had died.

Jack never set his alarm. He woke up naturally at seven. This morning, he had slept until ten of eight. He had missed breakfast. He was late for morning prayer.

He threw on his clothes and raced out the door, clattering down the steps like a wild man. But he still got a cut slip. Cut slips were what they handed out at Braddington for all minor infractions, like being more than five minutes late for assembly or class, more than one day late turning in an assignment. Ten cut slips in one semester and you were automatically expelled, as if you had fouled out of the game or something. This morning's cut was Jack's eighth. Something else to worry about.

Mens sana in corpore sano. Mr. Buecher, head of the phys.-ed. program, spoke about it as part of his morning address. *"Mens sana,"* he growled. *"Or wom-*

ens sana, as the case may be." He nodded to the girls' section, getting a big laugh.

He got an even bigger laugh and a loud cheer when he made beating Andover in this Friday's wrestling meet part of his morning prayer.

Mens sana. That was why daily gym was required. That was why you had to go out for a team. Even faculty was required to coach a sport. But Martin Rucker was such a weird kid that he received special dispensations that few other Braddington kids ever got. As far back as Jack could recall, no one had ever seen Martin *inside* the gym.

That was part of the reason Jack looked forward to wrestling practice today. At least, for one hour, he would be safe from Rucker.

He was in the middle of a takedown drill when he spotted Martin sitting high up in the bleachers.

Martin waved with both hands.

"He knows, right?" Cameron said.

"Yeah."

"He saw you?" asked Dede. The concern in her soft doe eyes was soothing, but not soothing enough.

"Yeah," Jack said.

"So?" said Bradford.

"So he's making all kinds of threats," Jack answered. He kept turning around to scan the crowded dining hall. He had spread word for his friends to meet him at Buford for dinner, instead of Carmichael, to try to give Martin the slip. He didn't know how long it would be before Martin figured out the ruse and caught up with him.

"What kind of threats?" Bradford asked.

"If I don't do what he says, then he'll tell Simmons."

Bradford nodded in that bulldog way of his; Jack could tell he was furious, which was something of a relief. He didn't really know what Bradford could do to Martin that he couldn't do himself, but he still liked having a big bear like Knox on his side. With a bodyguard like Bradford, what could go wrong?

"I'm going to fix it for you," Bradford promised.

"How?"

"I'm going to crack his head open like a coconut."

"I want to watch," Hunt drawled. "I'd like to see what's inside."

"He must have a computer in there," Cameron said, wiping his mouth with the paper napkin from Brooke's tray. "He's in my English class. Total genius. He's read everything."

"Oh, that's so sympathetic, Cameron," Brooke said. "The guy's torturing Jack, you want to talk about how well-read he is." She turned back to Jack. "So where's your little townie friend tonight?"

"I told you, don't call her that," Jack said, his eyes flashing.

"Sorrrry," Brooke said. "I just think it's kind of strange, you know, that you're going through this by yourself."

"I'm not doing it by myself," Jack said. "Now you just lay off her, understand?"

Brooke—always riding him—ever since—

"Jill eats dinner at home," Cameron told Brooke. "She's a day student, remember?"

"Here's what we do, Jack," said Hunt. "We spread the word. Everyone puts the heat on this geek meister. I bet we could make him so crazy he'll off himself once and for all."

"Oh, Hunt," said Dede, obviously shocked.

"What?" Hunt asked Dede. "The only good scuzzball is a dead scuzzball."

69

"I love it when you talk dirty," Brooke told Hunt, putting on a fake southern accent.

There was one rumor about Martin Rucker that happened to be totally true. He had once tried to kill himself. First year. He had hanged himself with a long string of school ties. But he had only succeeded in pulling down the light fixture and knocking himself unconscious. Mr. Simmons had found him. He'd spent the next semester at some mental hospital.

"What do you say, Jack?" Hunt asked. He made a fist and pounded his palm with it. "Green light?"

Jack shook his head. "NG."

"Why?"

"Because, first of all, I don't think Rucker cares about getting picked on. In fact, I think he gets off on it. Big victim complex. That's one." Jack looked around.

"What do you keep looking around for?" Bradford asked.

"He's got me thinking he's right behind me," Jack said.

"He's not here," Cameron assured him.

"Have you tried talking to him?" Dede asked.

Hunt smacked his head with the palm of his hand. "Dede, you're a genius. Why didn't any of us think of that?"

"Hunt," Bradford rumbled, "there's no call for being nasty."

"Bradford's right," Jack agreed.

Dede stared off in the direction of the chocolate-milk machine, so that no one would see her eyes water, probably. Jack's heart went out to her. It wasn't just sympathy. There had been more than one period when he'd wanted to go out with Dede. And vice versa. The timing had never worked out, was all.

"Guys," Cameron said sternly, "we don't have the time to fight right now. Jack needs our help."

Dede nodded. "That's right," she said.

"Okay, here's the deal," said Jack. "If we lean on him, he'll go crying right to Simmons."

"He won't," Hunt said. "He'd be too scared."

"No, he will," Jack said; there was a tightness in his chest, as if Martin had his hand in there and was squeezing. "I mean, look at it from his point of view. What's he got to lose?"

"Jack," Cameron said. "I just had an idea. We set him up."

"Set him up?"

"Yeah, you know, plant something in his room. Drugs, whatever. Then I tell Simmons I suspect him, we go up and search the place. Boom. He's out of here within a week."

"Right," Jack said. "And what do you think he does after he cleans out his room? He blabs." He held his head with both hands, trying to press the headache back inside. Somehow he had hoped that his friends could help him out of this one, but the more he thought about it, the clearer it became. There was no way out. He was at crazy Martin's mercy.

He got up from the table.

"You're going?" Brooke asked. She made a pouting expression with her lips.

"You haven't eaten anything," Dede said.

"Look who's talking," Bradford told her.

"Martin's probably waiting for me back at Carmichael," Jack said. "I wouldn't want to miss eating with him. Ha-ha." His friends were all looking at him; he wished he could just stay and relax and pal around with them like usual. But he couldn't. He was alone.

And Jill? The person he wanted to be with most? Right now he was dreading running into her almost as much as Martin. He'd promised Jill this would all be okay. He'd promised he'd call her back. Two lies. He'd avoided her all day.

"Listen, guys. Promise me no one touches Rucker. No one does anything even slightly mean to him. Okay? Maybe I can ride this thing out."

Maybe.

CHAPTER 10

THAT NIGHT, JILL SENT JACK TWO DESPERATE
E-mail messages. He didn't answer either one. Then
came a knock at the door. He had a phone call downstairs. Jack pretended he wasn't in his room.

Not only was he there, he wasn't alone. Martin
was with him, and had been since check-in, hanging
out as if they were roommates. Chattering happily
away.

The next morning, Jack tried to slink out of his
room without being noticed, but Martin threw open
his door, all set to join him. When you slept in your
clothes, you could get ready in a hurry. Martin followed Jack to breakfast and didn't shut up once the
whole way.

Jack had always hated morning prayer. But after
breakfast with Martin, he went to the rotunda, relishing
the idea of a few minutes' peace.

It was only after the sermon had started that he
turned and saw Martin sitting right next to him.
Martin winked. "I switched with Wallace," Martin
whispered. "Don't tell on me, okay?"

It was another horrible day spent ducking Jill

ERIC WEINER

and Martin both. That night, he got another E-mail message:

JACK—PLEASE! WE'VE GOT TO TALK! I'M GETTING REALLY FREAKED. PLEASE!!! CALL ME!!!!!—JILL

Jack turned off the computer. He just couldn't face her, not right now. He had to figure a way out of the Martin problem. Then he'd call her.

Jack always went to sleep early on nights before a meet. "But I really need to talk," Martin whined when Jack told him he needed to crash.

It was as if Martin had forgotten all about the threatening awful things he'd said. If Jack was nice to him, Martin became totally friendly. And it didn't seem to matter to Martin that Jack was faking it. Fake was probably the closest thing to friendship Martin Rucker had ever known.

Jack decided to let Martin talk until eleven, which was official lights-out anyway. But Martin didn't stop there. He insisted on putting a towel under the door— the old dorm trick for throwing off Mr. Simmons on one of his late-night prowls. Martin talked on.

It was after two when Martin said, "Goodness, Jack, look at the time. Don't you need your rest for your wrestling match?"

Jack nodded silently. He was so tired he thought he might be having an out-of-body experience. Not far enough out of his body, though, because he could still hear Martin, babbling away.

And even after Martin had left, he couldn't sleep. He was too tired. Knowing that he needed his sleep this night more than any other only keyed Jack up even more.

*   *   *

Friday afternoon, Jack showed up at the gym early.

So did Martin.

Though Jack wasn't required to attend the JV pre-meets, he always did, stalking up and down beside the mat, yelling himself hoarse.

Martin sat by himself in the front row of the concrete seats as near to the team bench as possible. He didn't watch, though. He seemed to be preoccupied with a sign he was making. Jack didn't want to know what the sign said.

The JV team got their asses kicked. Jack knew it was going to be a long afternoon when the usually dependable Bucky Moss got pinned, in the first period no less. Then Beller got his neck twisted and lost on a default. Jack kept yelling. He felt so tired, he knew he should conserve some energy. On the other hand, if he sat down he thought he'd go right to sleep.

He kept glancing at Martin. The guy never looked up once. What was he writing? A novel?

The main auditorium of the Braddington gym was built sort of like a Roman amphitheater. Row after concentric row of stone steps rose up to the high domed ceiling. Students sat on these green cushions you picked up at the door. As big as it was, the place filled up for the varsity meet. Both sides of the gym were packed, and the huge stacks of seat cushions dwindled down to nothing. It looked like several hundred Andover fans had made the trip.

Jack was leading his team warm-up when he caught sight of Jill. She was among the crowd still filing in. The gym had this huge beautiful skylight with all these championship banners hanging down. The sunlight reflected off Jill's hair as if she were on fire. She waved. He watched her head for the stands.

Luckily Martin didn't spot her. At least there was that. She sat high up and to the right.

The varsity had a decent team this year. They weren't expected to beat Andover, but that had only fueled their desire. Little Nick Davies led off with a thirty-two-second pin that brought the house down, almost literally, it felt. The students were stomping their feet so hard in the stands, Jack expected the dome to collapse.

Then Schuyler Wattell lost on points in a dreary match where he got behind early, and then just let the match slip away. That quieted down the Braddington side beautifully.

Jack's heart was racing. The score of the meet kept going back and forth, but mostly back. Two thirds of the way through, they were down by ten points.

Not insurmountable. But Stu Ferguson was wrestling some powerhouse from Andover named Walt Pickell, and getting rubbed into the mat pretty good. Still, if Stu could keep from getting pinned, then Jack would only need to win on points for his team to be back in it. And if Jack could *pin,* they were golden.

Because after Jack, the lineup was rock solid—Cameron, Hunt, and Bradford. Cameron would outclass his opponent easily. Hunt knew more moves than anyone in the league. He would do his famous leg moves and tie up his man like a pretzel. Bradford would squash his opponent like a bug.

The gym was packed to capacity. Kids were lined up in the aisles, standing by the windows, sitting on the window ledges—everywhere. The place was jumping.

And then—

Jack spotted Martin sitting high up in the stands, sitting right next to Jill. And the way they were talking, like they were old friends or some—

76

The roar of the crowd turned him back to the action on the mat. Pickell had sunk a half nelson on Ferguson and had gotten it in there pretty well. He was prying Stu off the mat and turning him over steady, like he was opening a tin can.

Jack looked back into the stands, but now Martin was gone. Or was he just imagining things?

Just then Coach Michaels took a step over to where Jack was crouching. He slapped Jack's thigh with a rolled-up program. He didn't look down at Jack, just kept watching the wrestlers and calling out, "Up, Stu. Up. Head up!" But then, out the side of his mouth, he told Jack, "Get warmed up."

When Coach moved off, Jack cursed. Just what he needed. More pressure. Because if Stu got pinned, it meant that Jack *had* to win or his team was mathematically eliminated.

He stripped off his sweatshirt and sweatpants. Raced in place a few times. He crossed his legs and reached down to hold his ankles, slowly pulling his head all the way down until his nose touched his knees.

Then he heard the sickening thud as the ref slapped the mat with his palm. There was a roar from the crowd. It came from the Andover side. Jack kept stretching. He didn't look.

Bradford sauntered out to where he was standing. He turned around, offering Jack his massive back. Jack draped himself across his friend. Bradford gently bounced up and down, cracking Jack's back.

When Bradford dropped Jack back down on the gym floor, Jack caught a glimpse of big Bill Dennehy pacing up and down on the Andover side of the mat. He already had his white plastic helmet tightly chin-strapped on. His hands were locked together and he was pulling his arms straight back, bulging the biceps.

"Murder him," Bradford instructed Jack. He had that somber look he always got during meets. Jack knew the look well. When Bradford was in this state, it meant he needed to tear someone limb from limb.

"Jack!" Bradford said to him sharply. "Where's your head? Don't look over there."

Jack was looking at the front row of the Braddington seats. Martin was back in his old spot—if he'd ever left it. And seeing Jack looking his way, he jumped to his feet, waving a sign.

LOOK OUT, ANDOVER, HERE COMES OUR JACK OF ALL TRADES. GOOOO, JACKIE!

Martin was shouting out a high-pitched cheer.

"The loser of all time," Jack muttered.

Bradford grabbed Jack's face in one big paw. "Look at me. He's nothing. You hear me, Jack? Nothing!" Then he moved his head closer so that he could be heard over the crowd. They had started stomping in anticipation of Jack's bout. "Imagine that it's him," Bradford instructed him.

"What?"

"Dennehy. Imagine that it's Rucker."

Jack nodded. Good idea. But his body felt all rubbery.

The ref blew his whistle. Dennehy danced out to the starting circle like a pony, shadowboxed, pumped his fists in the air. Boos from Braddington, cheers from Andover.

Then Jack stepped into the ring.

The greeting was thunderous.

He had always loved that cheer, the way it burst in your ears. He used to ride it like a wave. But today, when the roar began to subside, he heard Martin's shrill cry piecing the rest.

"You can do it, Jack!"

He and Dennehy stood on opposite sides of the

78

circle, trying to psych each other out with evil stares. Dennehy had a sour look on his face. It was a look of such utter hatred, it was unnerving. Jack was thinking about what Bradford had said. Think of Dennehy as Rucker. Bradford was right. *This* was what was behind Martin's mask—all this hate.

The ref gave a short blast on his whistle and waved his hands once, indicating the wrestlers should shake. Dennehy charged forward before Jack could even move. He clasped Jack's hand with an iron grip.

Then they took their positions again.

A longer blast on the whistle this time.

It brought the crowd to a thunderous silence.

And then the match began.

Dennehy came right at him, slapping Jack's arms, his face, trying to get a grip.

"Downstairs, Jack!" he heard Coach Michaels yell. "Downstairs, boy! Downstairs!"

Which was Coach's not-so-subtle way of telling Jack to drop to one knee and grab Dennehy's leg.

"I'm praying for you, Jackie!" That was Martin's contribution, now easily heard in the hush of anticipation.

Titters of laughter from both sides of the room.

And then—

It was Dennehy who heeded Coach's instructions. He suddenly dropped to one knee and lunged forward, grabbing Jack's legs. He got both of them, too, which was deadly, because he was holding them together. Jack couldn't balance, and the next thing he knew, they were flying backward. The only move Jack could hope to make in this position was baby-step backward so fast that he made it outside the white circle so the takedown didn't count.

He made it outside the circle. They were booking.

And Dennehy didn't let go. The ref blew his whistle as Jack came slamming down with Dennehy on top of him. Jack's head missed the hardwood floor with only inches to spare. Another whistle. The ref had awarded Jack two points for Dennehy's unsportsmanlike conduct.

Only a smattering of applause from the Braddington crowd—though, of course, frantic shrieks of joy from Martin. The only geek in the entire crowd who didn't know that that wasn't the way you won a wrestling match—by letting your opponent beat up on you too severely.

They came back to the circle to start again. Jack felt like about half the wind had been knocked out of him. Which wasn't good. Because he hadn't had all his wind to begin with and—

Dennehy was grinning now. Not a full grin. More of a sneer.

And then the ref blew his whistle again and—

Jack hit the first locker he came to, pounding on it with his fist. Then he found an empty locker with an open door and started banging that door back and forth, making an incredible racket. Enough noise to bring Mr. Moriarty, the maintenance man, running around the corner to see what was up. Jack ignored him. And when Moriarty saw who it was, he slunk off.

There was a muffled cheer from the gym, the crowd applauding as Cameron won what was now a meaningless match.

Jack ripped off his helmet, flinging it across the room. All the energy he hadn't felt out on the mat was coming back to him now. He kicked a bench over. Another, and another. Then he bent down, picked a bench back up, and slammed it down as hard as he could. Then he caught a glimpse of himself in the mirror. He could barely recognize his face, it was so red. Some of that was mat burn. Most of it was—

He roared. The sound ripped out of him with primal rage.

Not only had he lost. Dennehy had pinned him.

Jack heard a noise. A familiar throat clearing. He whirled.

"Jack," Martin said, "I thought you might be feeling kind of low after the way the match went, so I—"

"Rucker!"

Jack raced toward him. The boy turned and ran. And Jack, running after him, tripped over one of the benches he had just knocked over. He went down, shouting in agony, swearing wildly. Then he limped to his feet and took off after Martin.

But when he came out into the wide concrete hallway, he caught only a glimpse of Martin's gray suit as the boy hurried around the hallway's next bend. He ran after him. But when he turned the corner, he almost crashed into—

Brooke and Dede. The two girls both looked so concerned—it only made him madder. He tried to push them out of the way, but they shrieked and held their ground.

"Jack," Dede gasped, "are you okay? They can hear you all the way in the gym, yelling like that."

Jack took big gulps of air. There was sweat running off his nose. He tried to get past them, but Brooke wouldn't budge. "Out of my way!" Jack barked.

But they didn't move, and with each passing second, Jack could feel the rage leaving him. Pain and despair were rushing in to take the anger's place.

Which was lucky. Because if he had caught Rucker

just then, he'd have twisted his head right off his skinny little neck.

Truly.

He'd have killed him.

CHAPTER 11

EVERY THURSDAY AFTERNOON AT FIVE, THE faculty of Braddington held a meeting. Who knew what they talked about? Ways to make the students' lives more miserable, presumably. But if a student was up for expulsion, the Thursday meeting was when they voted on his case.

And this Thursday, almost a week after the wrestling match, the faculty was meeting to decide the fate of a senior who had snuck a girl into his room.

As was the custom among Braddington students, during the faculty meeting, the accused student and his friends—and in this case, they were numerous—all gathered on the roof of the administration building. From there you could see down into the quad. When the meeting ended, the accused student's faculty adviser would come out into the quad and give the students on the roof a thumbs-up or a thumbs-down.

If it was thumbs-up, there was wild cheering and jumping and shouting that, Jill had once told Jack, could be heard in downtown Braddington.

If it was thumbs-down, there was crying and wailing

as all the students hugged the friend who would soon be leaving them.

This Thursday was bleak to begin with, a slate-gray day in early December when the wind was raw and icy, grinding tiny particles of sleet into your face like glass. Jack, standing on the edge of the parapet, made no effort to shield himself. In fact, he stuck his face into the wind.

His heart was in his throat, and that was the truth.

There was a cry from the students. Jack opened his eyes into the stinging wind, looking down. The faculty were pouring out of the meeting. From this height, the teachers all looked appropriately puny, considering what they had probably just done.

The faculty adviser, Mr. Simmons, separated himself from the crowd and waved until he got the attention of the roof crowd. Several students waved back.

Then everyone waited with a stillness like awe.

Mr. Simmons held up his signal.

Thumbs-down.

And then the crying and the wailing began.

When Mr. Simmons gave the sign, Jack felt his stomach flip. He just stood there, feeling hollow and shell-shocked. Feeling almost nothing at all.

When he turned from the edge of the roof, he saw Jill, walking slowly toward him, her head down. He walked to meet her, wrapping an arm around her shoulder. She was crying.

And then Bucky Moss came loose from the crowd and hurried straight to Jack. Bucky threw his strong arms around his neck. "I'm going to miss you, Captain," he said.

CHAPTER 12

"I'LL MISS YOU, TOO," JACK TOLD BUCKY.

Bucky had been booted, tossed, kicked out, eighty-sixed—and for what? The exact same sin that Jack and Jill had committed. There but for the grace of Martin go I, thought Jack bitterly.

Jill's skin was red and raw from the wind and sleet. She wiped her nose with the back of her pink mitten. "I hate this place," she told Jack. He pulled her closer, trying to shield her face with his coat.

Beside him, Martin stood shivering bitterly in his overly long topcoat. Looking down at the top of Martin's brown head, Jack had the absurd feeling that this strange twisted creature was somehow his son—his and Jill's. They were with him often enough.

Jill had insisted that Jack had been imagining things when he asked what she and Martin had been talking about at the wrestling meet. Well, he hadn't been imagining things since then. Martin never left either one of them alone.

"To throw a student out like that," Martin said, his teeth chattering. "And for what? The natural urges of adolescence? It goes against nature, really. But come,

85

let's get out of the cold. We're going to Chez Henri tonight, my treat. Oh, and don't worry, there will be no repeats from yesterday or the day before. This time I absolutely positively won't forget my wallet!"

"What are we going to do? Jack?"

"I don't know."

"We have to do something," said Jill. "This is killing us. You know that, don't you? This is eating us alive."

It was Saturday afternoon. They were sitting in one of the five soundproof practice booths at the Music Center, where Jill played piano. The booths were these strange white metal boxes where you had privacy except for the thick glass door.

For once they were alone.

They were both sitting on the piano bench, but Jill had stopped playing a long time ago. She stretched her fingers over the keys, then made a fist, about to slam it down. Jack grabbed her hand. She waited for him to say something. He could see the pain in her face and he hated it.

"Hey," he said. "You finally played for me, Rabbit."

No response.

"Jill . . . after this spring, we're out of here. Then he's got nothing on us."

"Spring? We'll never make it."

"Sure we will."

"He keeps upping his demands, Jack."

It was true. Two days ago, he had demanded that Jack and Jill let him share their carrel in the library. Yesterday afternoon, he had made Jack buy him a whole batch of new clothes. Then Martin wanted to hang his clothes in Jack's closet. When Jack complained, Martin said that his own room was too messy to store such fine things, "And besides, what's mine is yours, right, Jack?"

"Jack," Jill said.

"Yeah."

"You're like a million miles away."

"Am I?"

"Brooke talked to me at lunch today. She says she's going to switch dining halls if Martin keeps eating with everybody."

"Well, that would be a big loss," Jack said. He laughed bitterly. "You want to hear something sick? I saw her and Hunt making out behind Whitman last night, right before check-in."

"No! Does Cameron know?"

"No. I don't know. He's always suspicious of her, you know."

Suddenly Jack turned and stared back out the glass door of the booth. He could see a girl lugging a double bass toward the orchestra rehearsal space.

"What?" Jill asked.

"It's amazing," Jack said. "But I think this is the first time I've forgotten about Rucker—really forgotten about him, you know?—in I don't know how long."

Jill chewed thoughtfully on a luscious lock of her strawberry-blond hair. "Jack? Why does he hate you so much?"

Jack felt that old clammy-sweaty feeling. It was a question he'd been dreading for a while.

"Why do you say he hates me?"

"Jack—he's torturing you. What do you call that?"

"Mean?"

"Jack—"

"It's totally crazy. I mean, I'm the only one who was ever nice to the creep." Jack felt himself blushing. "What? What are you looking at me like that for?"

But he knew why. She was looking at him because she knew he was holding out on her.

She always knew.

He tapped out a low note on the piano. Waited as the vibrations slowly settled.

"Tell me, Jack," she demanded.

But he didn't say a word.

"Jack—"

All of a sudden—and it came as much as a surprise to Jack as it did to Jill—he straight-punched the front of the piano with all his might. The top of the baby grand slammed down hard, rattling several notes at once. Jack's hand throbbed wildly. "I've never told anyone before," he lashed out, "okay?"

Her eyes had widened. To Jack, it felt as if a mask had dropped, and for a moment he had shown her the real Jack Washburn.

He put the mask back on as quickly as he could.

"Are you out of your mind?" she asked.

"I'm just a little on edge—"

"Why don't you get an ax and hack the piano to pieces. That way we'll be sure not to call attention to ourselves."

"Jill, I'm sorry. It's just something I don't exactly like talking about, okay? But—all right, all right, all right!—here's the whole story."

And then he told her.

How in their first form, Martin lived in the room right across from Simmons's apartment. Simmons had hated Rucker right off the bat. Not too surprising, the way Martin was always saying that crazy "If you would, kind sir" stuff and all. In short order, Martin became the dorm scapegoat. Everyone was making fun of him, chanting his name when he walked by, the whole bit.

"Don't look at me like that," Jack said. "I was

88

one of the very few kids who would even talk to him. I was just in my first year, remember. What was I supposed to do? Beat up all the big kids? One time, I saw some seniors going in Martin's room to trash the place, I yelled like hell until Simmons came."

Jill was smiling at him, as if to say, "That's my Jack." Well, she wouldn't be smiling long, he thought.

"I got plenty of flak for that, believe me. If I hadn't been on JV football, I probably would have become an outcast like Rucker."

"Not you, Jack."

"Then one day I run into Martin in the bathroom. He's crying. It was an awful sight. I mean, he was yelping like a dog when it gets hit by a car. His whole body shaking. He's wearing one of those ridiculous suits of his. I just felt so sorry for him. I let him cry on my shoulder. He told me it was his birthday, and that his parents both forgot to call."

"He was crying so hard about *that?*"

"Jill, you're from a regular family. You don't know what it's like."

"Regular family? That's a laugh. Someday I'll let you come over and you'll never want to go out with me again."

"That's not true, and you know it. Listen, the point is, your family is still together. Look, Jill . . . I get occasional postcards from my mom in Europe, okay? I see my dad as infrequently as possible. I think I know what Martin was going through. You've heard Martin's stories. Believe me, neither of his parents want him, that's a given. He's like nothing to them. So the birthday thing, something like that, it just reminds him of how little they care."

"You're right." She leaned over and gave him a gentle kiss. "I love you, by the way," she said.

He didn't answer. Let her say that when he finished. "So the guy is bawling his eyes out and I can't think of how to help him and I think he's going to have a nervous breakdown or something and it's tearing at my heart. So I finally say, 'Martin. Wash your face, we're going out to eat. I'm taking you out for your birthday. Chez Henri. Sky's the limit.'"

"Jack—why didn't you tell me any of this before?"

"Because I'm telling you now."

"We said no secrets, Killer."

"You want to hear it or not?"

She rubbed a white piano key, thinking. "So that's why when he sat down with us that first time at Chez Henri, he said, 'Seems like old times'?"

Jack didn't answer.

Jill nodded thoughtfully. "Go on."

"Well, you should have seen him. You can imagine how happy he got. By the time we got to the restaurant, he was squealing. Heads were turning, believe me. Martin probably had the best time he's ever had. I had the worst lunch I've ever had in my whole life. But the thing is, after that? Well, let's just say . . . my little plan backfired."

Jill laughed lightly. He knew what she was thinking about. It wasn't the first time a plan of his had gone awry.

"After that," he said, "Martin wanted to hang with me *constantly*."

"Sounds familiar."

"Yeah, only you know what? In some ways, it was worse back then, because I was a first former. I was fourteen. To be seen with Martin, it was like the most humiliating thing in the world. I—I tried to let Martin down gently. I did. But whenever I would refuse to do something with him, he'd get

90

furious. Finally he stopped speaking to me altogether—which was no tragedy, as far as I was concerned. But then he stopped speaking to anyone, and—"

Jack broke off. There were tears in his eyes.

"Go on," Jill said, a little surprised. "I want to hear it all."

Jack waited until the lump in his throat had gone back down before he spoke. "He just snapped, Jill. I mean, that's when he started staying up all night, every night. But not just for a few nights, for a whole week. And he stopped eating. It was awful."

He choked up again. He couldn't tell anymore. Jill squeezed his hand.

"And?"

"And then he killed himself. Tried to anyway."

Jack wiped furiously at his eyes with the back of his hand.

"Jack."

"Yeah."

"You didn't do anything wrong. You're not blaming yourself for that, are you?"

Jack shuddered. In a low voice, he went on. "One week later, after Mr. Simmons found him? Mr. Rucker showed up and helped Mr. Simmons clean out Martin's room. Mr. Simmons introduced me as a close friend of Martin's. I had to shake his father's hand."

"Well, if you want to blame someone, Jack, blame that father. Don't blame yourself."

"I wasn't there for him, Jill! Can't you understand what that feels like? Maybe if I'd talked to him more, I could have—"

"Jack, that hospital they sent him to—it probably has all these top shrinks, right? Were *they* able to help him? Were they?"

"I guess not." Jack nodded gratefully. He was loving her more than ever. "He sure isn't any better as far as I can tell."

"Not any better at all," agreed Martin.

CHAPTER 13

WHO KNEW HOW LONG HE HAD BEEN listening? He must have opened the door inch by inch. He had stuck his head inside the booth. He was smiling.

Jill gasped. But the craziest thing of all? Jack wasn't that surprised to see him. Martin had snuck up on him too many times these past few weeks. It was getting to be more surprising to him when Martin *wasn't* there.

But that wasn't all. In a way, he had meant for Martin to hear everything.

"I'm glad you're here, Martin," Jill said.

"Oh, really? Somehow I doubt that." Martin stepped into the booth, closing the door behind him. He picked nervously at his badly chapped lips.

"Is that why you're doing this?" Jill asked him. "Because you're still mad at Jack for what happened first year?"

They both looked at Martin, waiting. Martin seemed deep in thought. Jack suddenly felt hopeful. He had confessed, to Jill—and as it turned out, to Martin as well. Maybe Martin would let it go at last.

Then Martin smiled. It was an angry and disgusting smile, and it made Jack's heart sink.

"What shall I play for you?" Martin asked. He rolled up the sleeves of his suit. "Seriously. You know I play like a demon!"

Everyone in school knew. One of the few times Martin liked to come out of his room was for orchestra rehearsals. He'd sit in the back of the room, eyes closed, listening. When rehearsal was over, he'd sit down at the piano, and as everyone was leaving he'd play the whole symphony, by ear, and from memory.

"Out of the way, my friends."

They stood, letting him sit at the piano bench. Martin started pounding the keyboard with his fists. Then he swiveled to face them. He grinned, that same furiously triumphant smile. "Rachmaninoff. Such a passionate composer, don't you think? Ha-ha. Just kidding."

And then he began to play Rachmaninoff for real.

Martin was telling the truth.

He did play like a demon.

Even though it was three in the morning, Jill answered on the first ring.

"It's me," Jack said.

"Hi."

"I hope I didn't wake you up."

"You didn't." She sure sounded wide-awake, wired in fact.

"What are you doing?"

"Working at the computer. What's wrong? Are you okay?"

"Yeah, yeah, I'm fine. Better than fine. I'm really fantastic, if you want to know the truth." He wasn't being sarcastic. He felt like he could breathe again, for the first time in weeks.

"And Martin?" Jill asked.

"What do you mean?"

"Is he okay, too?"

Jack tried to laugh. "Hey, what is that? Some kind of a joke? You're worrying about *him* now?"

"I worry about what you'll do to him, Killer."

Jack had always liked that nickname. Now it stung, despite his good mood. "Jill, you can knock off that Killer stuff, okay?" he said lightly. "I mean, seriously, let me ask you this. How many guys would have put up with what Martin has been pulling? I mean it. How many guys do you think would have the patience I've had?"

"Is he okay?"

"He's upstairs sleeping in my chair like a baby."

"Good."

He didn't want to argue. Didn't want to lose his momentum, his excitement. "Jill, I just had a brain-storm. I mean, I've thought this whole thing through a hundred different ways. I finally realized. There's only one way out."

"Suicide?"

"Close . . ." Jack waited, feeling dramatic. "We let him turn us in," he said at last.

"What!"

"What I mean is, we just drop him, cold. No more hanging out with him, no more lunches, no more late-night talks. We tell him if he wants to turn us in, go right ahead. He probably won't go to the dean anyway. And if he does? I'll lose my trust fund. Big deal. What's a million bucks?" Jack chuckled happily. He felt such relief, like someone had filled him with helium and let go of the string.

"Jack, that's easy for you to say."

"You're right," he agreed happily. "It is easy. I don't know why it took me so long to see it."

"Easy for *you*. Look, Jack, I don't want to be crass, but face facts. We're not in the same boat here. I mean, you *know* your father will never disown you altogether, no matter what you do."

"Ohhhhh, you don't know my father."

"Okay, let's say he does kick you out of the house. You're still a Washburn, right? With connections up the wazoo. What am I? A Marshack. And if I lose my scholarship, Jack, then I'm nothing. I'm right back where I started. I'll never get out of this little crap town. I couldn't face my family after that, Jack. They have such high hopes for me, you wouldn't believe it. If I don't end up president of the country or something, they're going to be disappointed. Imagine how they'll feel when I'm expelled. I'd die of shame."

"It would be bad, I agree," Jack said. He had thought this part out as well. "But here's what we do. We get married."

The quality of the silence on the other end of the line changed, got deeper somehow. "You don't mean that," she said.

"I do. We go off and get married. I've got *some* money. Like I could sell my Porsche, my Rolex. That would give us enough to get started right there. And we'd work hard, Jill, just like real people do, and we'd finish high school somewhere, you know, in a regular public school. And then we'd go to college, work our way through. And . . . I don't know, Jill. It might even be fun in a way. Probably be good for me, not to have everything handed to me on a silver platter. Learn the meaning of a dollar, like my dad always says—"

He stopped, pressing the receiver hard against his ear. "Jill? Rabbit?"

"You are the biggest fool I've *ever*—"

She was furious. Her voice was trembling. "You

think being poor is like what you see in the movies? You think it's fun? You think it's *good* for you?"

"Well, I—"

But he didn't finish the sentence. Because all at once his elation faded, like a mirage.

She was right. It was a stupid ludicrous plan. He saw that now. It was his worst plan ever. It would never work.

And that meant—they were back to square one.

CHAPTER 14

"I'VE GOT A SOLUTION," JACK WHISPERED TO Jill the next morning in Latin class.

"That's what you said last night," Jill reminded him.

"We're going to get away."

"Where? Argentina?"

Jack smiled ruefully. "I was thinking someplace more exotic. Groton, Connecticut."

It had come to him that morning during Reverend Morrissey's invocation. "As the semester comes to a close we're all under great pressures," she said in her oddly deep voice. "Pressures in our schoolwork, pressures in our friendships. Pressure. And I just want to remind you all that there is a whole world outside the four walls of Braddington. Not everything that goes on here is earth-shattering. Not to us, not to the world, and certainly not to our Father above."

Sitting up on stage, where he sat for every morning prayer, Dean Schmidt was frowning. The dean always frowned when anyone said anything that sounded like an excuse not to work all the time.

"So my prayer to all of us this morning," Reverend

Morrissey had concluded, "is that we take the time in these last seven days before Christmas break—"

Smiling, Reverend Morrissey waited for the wild applause to subside. She was a pale woman with hair that looked gray even though it wasn't. The stage lights were glinting off her glasses. "Take the time," she went on, as if there had been no interruption, "to relax. For even in the middle of a storm, there is an eye. Even in the middle of darkness, there is light. In hurry we must rest. Let us pray."

Jack had never prayed in his life. He prayed that morning. Prayed for some relief from Martin Rucker.

And then it came to him. A weekend away from campus might do him and Jill a world of good. The reverend was right. Surely they could put up with some crazy smelly kid's company. All they needed was an occasional break

"Personally," said Jack Washburn II, pausing to tap his lips with a cloth napkin, "I thought your dad should have received the Nobel Peace Prize for that truce he made . . . in Chad, wasn't it, Martin?"

"The Congo, sir."

"The Congo, yes, that's right, that's right." Mr. Washburn refilled his wineglass for the sixth time. "Mighty fine man, your father."

"Oh, I couldn't agree more."

Jill raised her eyebrows slightly. She was sitting across from Jack at the wide mahogany dining table that floated in the middle of a vast sea of a beige Persian rug. Hanging above them was a huge crystal chandelier, the kind of extravagant fixture that was more appropriate in the lobby of an opera house than a private home. Other than the dim light from the wall sconces, the chandelier's bright glow was the only light in the room. It always gave Jack the feeling that he was floating in midair, hovering above the carpet. He hated this room. But never more than tonight.

Martin, his scraggly hair freshly combed after a rare shower, sat right beside him, seeming somber and serious and cheerful and totally sane.

Whenever you left campus overnight, you had to have special permission from the dorm head. And you had to sign a checkout list in the common room so that the proctor knew not to look for you at check-in. To fool Martin, Jack had told Cameron to sign his name for him, after he had already left. But when he and Jill got to his car, Martin was already sitting in the backseat, smiling and waving like an eager puppy.

As he had explained proudly on the drive to Connecticut, Martin had fallen into the habit of hanging out in Jack's room, even when he wasn't around. He said he felt safer there, somehow. And he had just happened to notice that the suitcase was missing from Jack's closet.

"This is really delicious," Jill told Gilda, who was sitting at the head of the table, opposite her husband. Jill raised a spoonful of soup to her lips, but her hand was trembling. She put the spoon back down in her soup bowl.

"Thanks," Gilda answered in an offhand way that made Jill's face fall.

And then Martin was off again, beginning another one of his windbag speeches. Jack could feel the sweat beginning to bead on his forehead. "Jill's one of the top students in our class," he said abruptly.

"Jack," admonished his father, nodding at Martin, who was still blabbering on.

Jack tried to throw Jill as reassuring a look as possible. She looked lost. It would have been stressful

100

enough for her, coming to a house like this, meeting his parents. Stressful enough without Martin.

Gilda must have pressed the buzzer at her foot, because Debby, the maid, suddenly hurried in.

"Yes, ma'am?"

Gilda waved one beringed hand. "Clear the soup, Debby, we're ready for the main course now."

"Yes, ma'am."

"We've been sitting here forever," Gilda told her, smiling slightly. "I shouldn't have to buzz you every time."

The witch. The stepmonster, thought Jack as Debby, head bowed, started clearing the large silver soup tureen and Lalique crystal bowls. Gilda had been a mere secretary at the bank before she snared his millionaire father. She had begun her affair with him while Jack's parents were still married. Now she put on airs as if she came from the oldest money in the world.

Well, for once, there was someone at the table that Jack hated more than Gilda.

Martin had launched into yet another story, all about how close he and his father were, how they planned to travel together this summer, go orangutan watching in Borneo, visit the pope in Rome, that sort of thing. *Right.* "But, oh dear me," Martin said, "I'm monopolizing the conversation. You and your wife must want to hear all about Jill."

"Well, now that you mention it," Mr. Washburn said, turning to Jill with a smile.

"Now, at school, Jill is what we call a townie," Martin went on. "It's a nasty term, I'm afraid, but if ever there was proof that the whole townie concept was unfair—you're looking at her. A fine, fine young lady, and don't let anyone tell you different, right, Jack?"

101

Jill tried to laugh, but she was in such pain it came out sounding more like a yelp. Mr. Washburn reddened. His temper was more famous than Jack's. Jack suddenly wished that Mr. Washburn would throttle Martin for him; Martin couldn't blame him for that.

"Martin," Mr. Washburn began in a low voice, "I don't think that's the kind of talk we want at our dinner table, now is it?"

"Oh, no, sir," Martin agreed humbly. "I mean, that's my point, sir. It just upsets me so much when students talk that way. I always tell them to stop it."

"Good."

"But," Martin said. "They don't stop. Townie, townie, townie, it's like every other word out of their mouth is—"

"That's enough," Jack said in a voice that didn't sound like his own. He said it straight across the table at Jill, as if he weren't talking to Martin at all.

There was a profoundly awkward silence.

"Mr. Washburn," Jill said, "Jack tells me that you also used to, uh, um, wrestle at, uh, er, Braddington?"

Her voice sounded so pinched and strained. She was probably scared out of her mind, finding herself in such a rich house; she was trying to speak so politely, but it just came out sounding silly.

"Oh, yeah," Mr. Washburn said, nodding. He flexed a muscle. "Bet I could still take Jack here. What do you say, huh, Jack? Think I could take you?"

"Fight, fight," chanted Martin, clapping. He guffawed. Then he reached out and touched Mr. Washburn's arm, leaning forward to add as if privately, "Don't bring up wrestling with Jack right now. I'm afraid it's rather a sore subject."

"Oh?"

Martin lowered his voice to a stage whisper. "Last meet. Andover? He got pinned."

Mr. Washburn chuckled. "Pinned? That's a first, now isn't it, Jack?"

"Oh dear," said Gilda, tittering like this was somehow hysterical.

"You know, Martin," said Mr. Washburn, "if you look on the wall of the trophy room at the gym, you'll see my picture. Our team was undefeated. Eleven and 0. I won't tell you the year, though, I don't want to shock you."

"I should look in the mid-1970s, I suppose," said Martin, gazing at the chandelier.

Mr. Washburn looked pleased. "Earlier than that, I'm afraid."

"Oh, my, you certainly don't look it, sir."

In many ways, Mr. Washburn was a carbon copy of Jack, especially around the eyes. His hair was silver, though, and his face red and creased from two many summers out on his yacht with everyone except Jack's mother. And right now his eyes were bloodshot from too much wine. He was forty-eight. He looked about ten years older than that.

"Jack, I'm glad you brought Martin home to visit us," Mr. Washburn said, opening another wine bottle. "Shows us your tastes are broadening, for once."

Jack cut a glance at Jill, whom his father had seemed to have totally written off. She was looking down at her plate. "Dad," Jack began, "I don't think I told you, but Jill finished third this semester in—"

"It gets tiresome," Mr. Washburn continued to Martin, overriding the interruption, "after a while, meeting only Jack's jock friends. I like jocks, myself. Hell, I am one. But unlike Jack here, I also crave intellectual stimulation. That's why I sent Jack to Braddington in the first place. Try to get that noodle of his working for once."

103

"Jill got a seven-seventy on her math SAT," Jack blundered on, "and last year she was voted—"

"Jack!" Jill said it sharply enough to stop him mid-sentence. Mr. Washburn looked over at Jill as if he had forgotten she was there.

"You don't have to do that," Jill said. "I can . . . speak for myself."

Martin's eyes twinkled merrily. "Jill's very modest," he told the whole table. "She doesn't want Jack to brag. But perhaps she'll allow me to do the honors." Martin smiled at Jack's parents. "May I say that in all my years, I've never met a more upstanding, morally fine person than Jill Marshack. Now, as I'm sure you know, the faculty of Braddington is very worried about boys sneaking girls into their dorm rooms— ha-ha—but if all the students were like Jill? Well! They wouldn't have to worry."

Jill dropped her knife with a clatter onto her plate.

"I mean, if you think for one second that Jack and Jill here would ever—"

Jack's fist hit the table hard enough to make the silverware jump.

"Jack!" Gilda gasped.

"Oh, I'm afraid you'll have to cut Jack a little slack, as they say," Martin said. "He's been under a terrible strain lately. He stays up to all hours and can't seem to buckle down and hit the books. I'm rather worried about him actually."

Jack pushed back from the table.

"Jack, where are you going?" Gilda asked sharply.

"I thought I'd help Debby serve the roast," he said as meanly as he could.

Gilda blinked several times, the way she did when she was angry. "Debby doesn't need help. She *is* the help. Sit down."

"Yes, *Mother*."

"Don't use that tone with your stepmother, Jack," Mr. Washburn said sternly.

Gilda said to her husband, "Are you going to let him get away with this?"

"Jack," his father said, obeying Gilda's orders as usual, "please." He glowered at Jack. Jack could tell by the set of his jaw just how mad he was. Nothing made him madder at Jack than Gilda being angry at *him*.

And then Martin started giggling. He went on giggling until everyone was staring at him. "I'm sorry," he said. "Private joke."

"No, come on . . . what is it?" Mr. Washburn insisted. Martin laughed so long that Mr. Washburn finally started to laugh along with him.

"I was just thinking," Martin said, "excuse me"—he covered his mouth, as if trying to stop more giggles— "oh dear, so funny. No, I was just thinking, how here you're getting so mad at Jack just for acting a little rude at the table. When if you only knew—"

"What was that?" Mr. Washburn asked. "Knew what?"

Gilda's eyes lit up. With dollar signs, thought Jack. "What's he done?" she demanded. "Jack," she told her husband. "You know the agreement. If he's done something wrong—"

Mr. Washburn made a sucking sound with tongue and tooth. Then he raised his large head, staring straight at Jack. "What is it this time, Jack? I won't bail you out again, Jack, you know that, don't you? Now what have you done?"

"Nothing," Jack said, almost pleading.

"Nothing at all," Jill agreed. There were little red splotches on her cheeks, as if she'd been slapped.

"Now, why don't I believe that?" Gilda said, rolling her eyes.

"What did Martin mean?" Mr. Washburn demanded.
"I really don't know," Jack said. His voice broke.
And through it all, Martin was cackling.

CHAPTER 15

"I HAVE NEVER BEEN SO HUMILIATED IN ALL my—"

"Jill—"

"They hated me! What am I saying? They didn't even think enough of me to hate me. It was like I didn't exist, like I—"

"Jill, listen—"

Jack had her by the arms, shaking her, but he couldn't make her stop.

"I don't belong here, Jack."

"That's nonsense," he whispered fiercely, "the whole thing was—"

"I was like some crumb on the table, some dirt that the maid could sweep up after the meal."

"Jill!"

They were in the butler's pantry off the dining room. Jack could hear the maids clearing the table. But more important, he could hear Martin singing in the powder room. They didn't have much time.

"The whole thing was Martin's fault," he whispered. "Martin, Martin, Martin. They would love you if they met you on their own. And anyway, who cares what they think? They're awful people, I told you. Just 'cause they have money doesn't mean they're not jerks! Jill! Wait a minute! Jill!"

She had pulled free. She ran out the back of the pantry and into the den.

And the worst thing of all, he didn't feel like going after her.

The one good thing about Jack's father's estate—it was big. Three floors. Ten bedrooms. And ten bathrooms, not counting the two toilets in the basement for the servants. You could get lost in a house like that. And that's just what Jack did. If Jill was going to run off, so could he. Let the maids show Jill and Martin to their rooms, he told himself. He was out of there.

He roamed the third floor for hours. There were secret places in that house, and after years of exploring as a child, Jack knew them all. The storage room behind the study. The little room off the stairs on the way up to the attic. Jack had the home-field advantage now, he thought. Martin could never find him here.

But it wasn't enough to be away from Martin, he discovered. It wasn't enough to be away from his parents and Jill. He had to get away from himself. And he knew only one way to do that. He ended up on the sofa in the third-floor library, guzzling bourbon straight from the bottle.

About halfway through the bottle, things began to get a little hazy. Three quarters of the way through the bottle, he . . .

"Poor fool."
"Don't call him that."

"In there, sleeping like a baby. Snoring, even."

"Martin, please"—Jill tried to keep her hatred and disgust out of her voice—"I've had a very difficult night, so if you don't mind . . ."

"Don't mind what?"

She was lying under the pink coverlet in the antique four-poster bed of one of the many guest rooms. Martin was sitting next to her, and the weight of his body was holding the covers tight around her, trapping her. He was fully clothed except for his black wing tips. He was working his fingers in between his toes, scratching hard through his gray socks. She looked away.

"You're seriously asking me to leave?" he asked quietly.

She could never loathe someone as much as she loathed Martin, she realized.

"I thought," Martin said, "that we had an understanding."

"We do, but it's one in the morning and—"

"And what? We'll all turn into pumpkins?"

Jill shuddered. He wiped his hands against each other. "Athlete's foot," he told her. "What a curse."

Then he put a hand to his mouth. He giggled happily.

"What?" she said.

"Jack's asleep."

"Yeah. So?"

"We're all alone. This may come as a shock to you, but I could count the number of times I've been alone with a girl on one hand."

Some shock.

"You look so cute," Martin said. "Jack's right. You're like a pretty little rabbit. Wiggle your nose for me, rabbit."

"Stop it!" she said sharply.

109

He inched his hand toward her bare arm, where it lay outside the covers.

She jerked her arm away.

He shook his head. "Jill," he said. And his eyes were suddenly dark. "I don't think you fully understand your . . . situation."

"Oh, I understand perfectly."

"No," he said. He put one hand on the pillow next to her, and used it to prop himself up as he slowly lowered his face close to hers. "No, you don't."

"Get away from me," she said, but she made no move to escape. He was moving his head closer. She could smell his fishy breath.

"Okay, Jill," Martin said softly, "I want you to think very carefully about what you do next. Because—"

Closer.

"The consequences . . ."

And now their lips were only inches apart.

"Could be—"

And then, to her everlasting disgust, he planted his mouth flush onto hers.

She shoved him back with both hands. Flinging off the covers, she jumped out of the bed. Even though Martin stayed on the bed, she backed up against the wall.

"You're crazy!" she spat out.

He looked a little scared by her anger, but he just shook his head. Slowly, sadly. And then he patted the bed with his hand.

Jack sat up quickly. A mistake. His head pounded. He looked around the room in a daze. There was his Braddington pennant on the wall. Some of his sports trophies. It struck him as a little boy's room. The room of a stranger.

He looked at his watch: 11:17. Oh, wow . . . he

110

had slept so late. Then he saw his sleeve—the sleeve of his dress shirt. He pulled back the sheets. He was fully clothed.

That was strange. Why would—

A few vague and nightmarish images flashed before him. Getting drunk. Guzzling the stuff. A late-night trip downstairs for more liquor. He had fallen. Yes . . . he could still feel the bruises. So he knew that part of his memory was true. And then . . . Jill . . . Jill and . . . Martin? They had helped him back upstairs, loosened his tie, taken off his shoes, gotten him back into—

He lurched to his feet, sticking them into his dress shoes without tying the laces. He shuffled into the bathroom, where he took one glance and one glance only at his disheveled face. It looked as if his skin had shifted, so that his eyes were no longer looking out of their sockets. He splashed himself with cold water, then hung his head over the sink for a long moment. The room was spinning. He thought he was going to puke.

The house struck him as ominously quiet as he came down the carpeted front stairs.

"Jill!" he called.

No response.

There was a pot of coffee brewing on the kitchen stove. He pulled a mug out of the cupboard and filled it. It was way too hot to sip. He inhaled some of the steam.

A maid he'd never seen before entered from the pantry, stopping short when she saw him.

"You must be Jack Junior," she said.

He didn't answer.

"Can I fix you some breakfast?"

"Where are my friends?"

"Your friends?"

"The tall girl with the reddish-blond hair. The weird kid with the—"

Then he heard him. Somewhere in the house. Martin was singing.

"Jack and Jill went up the hill to fetch a pail of waterrrrr!"

He sounded so happy. Happier than Jack had ever heard him.

Jack took a step—only one—out of the kitchen. The coffee sloshed over onto his hand, scalding him. He dropped the cup with a smash. The hot liquid splashed onto his legs, burning him again.

"It's okay," the maid said quickly. "I'll clean it."

Jack wasn't even listening. From where he was standing, he could see out the kitchen's bay windows.

The backyard of the Washburn estate was a long rolling snow-covered lawn that flowed down to the woods, pausing on its way to lap around a kidney-shaped pool (covered now for winter), a gazebo, and a sculpture garden. Sitting huddled in the gazebo, her hooded head hanging down, was Jill.

"Excuse me," Jack said, and even though it killed his head, he raced out the back door, without putting a coat on, across the snow-covered lawn.

Jill looked up when she saw him. She'd been crying. She was crying still.

He stood stock-still in front of her, not climbing the steps to the gazebo. The icy wind bit his face and ears. But his heart had stopped for another reason.

"What happened?" he asked.

She looked away.

Jack advanced up the slick wooden steps into the gazebo, slipping once on the ice.

"I said, 'What happened?'"

"Jack. He promised me—"

Jack stopped short.

"He promised me that he won't bother us anymore. He said that—"

Jack grabbed her harm, squeezing hard, hurting her. "Did he touch you?"

She didn't answer. She didn't have to.

"I'll kill him!" he cried. He turned to rush away but Jill caught his arm and held on, holding him back, begging him to stay.

"How could you!" he shouted at her.

"I-I-"

"How could you!" Jack was crying too, now, the tears stinging his cheeks as they rolled over his frozen skin.

"He kept pressuring me, telling me I had no choice . . . he said if I didn't, then he'd . . . destroy us . . . both. You and me, both."

Jack sank to his knees. His knees cracked down hard against the frozen wood of the gazebo floor. His hands covered his face. He was sobbing. She tried to pull his hands away, but he yanked his head away from her.

Finally he looked up. She looked blurry, because he was staring at her through a film of tears. "Tell me!" he cried.

"Tell you . . ." she echoed vaguely, "tell you what?"

"Everything!"

"Oh, Jack . . . no . . ."

"Everything!" He got back to his feet, slipping and sliding around the gazebo like a wild man. Jill gave a short scream when he started butting his head hard against one of the gazebo's white posts. "Tell me! How long was he . . . did he . . ."

"I don't know! About . . . four hours."

It felt like she had driven a stake into his brain. Jill's shoulders were heaving. "Jack, I swear to you, it was

113

the only way." Jack raised a hand over his head as if to slap her. "It was the *only way!*" she shouted at him, and then her mouth twisted, and fresh sobs shook her.

"He promised me, Jack," Jill said, weeping. "He gave me his solemn word. Don't you . . . see? I took care . . . of the problem, Jack. It's over." She nodded her head, repeating the words as if she were praying. "It's over."

But of course, that Monday, when they got back to school, Martin went back on his solemn word.

Back at school, Martin was as demanding as ever.

And now Jack had a new solution in mind.

CHAPTER 16

HE WAITED UNTIL SUNDAY NIGHT TO TELL HER. First he took her for a little spin in his silver Porsche, whipping around Braddington at dangerous speeds. Then he pulled into the 7-Eleven parking lot and killed the engine and the lights. He watched a couple of redneck townies come out of the store with two paper bags of groceries. They headed for their souped-up Jeep. Jack could see Wonder Bread and a six-pack of Bud poking out the top of one of the bags. He waited till their Jeep had driven off, then turned to her.

"Jill, I told you on the phone I had a plan. Now I don't want you to get all upset when you hear this, because believe me, I've thought this through. It's the only way. The *only* way."

Jill wasn't saying anything, wasn't helping at all. In a way, this was probably going to be the worst part, thought Jack. Saying the words out loud.

"We're going to get rid of Martin, Jill. We're going to off him."

"What are you talking about?"

"I'm talking about killing him."

Jill didn't react for a moment. Then she laughed.

In fact, she had such a fit of giggles that she had to pop the glove compartment and hunt around for a tissue to wipe her eyes and blow her nose. "You know what the worst part is?" she said finally. And now her laughter seemed to have turned without any break into a little crying jag. "The worst part is that he's probably going to turn us in anyway, no matter what we do. He'll get tired of torturing us and he'll want to play a new game."

"Exactly," Jack said.

And then—it was the most awful sight—he saw the look pass across her face as she realized that he was *serious*. He wasn't joking at all. She was sitting across from a murderer. He knew, right then, right in his gut, that she would never think of him the same way again.

"Go to hell," she said quietly.

He started the engine and pulled out of the parking lot, sending up a spray of gravel as he fishtailed back onto the road. They did three more laps around the town before either one of them said a word.

"Jill?"

"Yeah?"

Jack turned from the wheel and gave her a look, smiling tensely.

"Don't start that again," Jill said, her face drawn and pale. "If you bring it up again—I'm serious now, Jack—if you bring it up again to me, I will never speak to you."

"How do you know what I'm thinking about?" Jack asked.

There was a long silence. He kept his eyes on the road. He almost gave up hope that she would answer, then she said:

"Because I'm thinking about it, too."

116

"Good. Look, I've thought this out very carefully."

"Oh, Jack, *please.*" Jill's green eyes were dark with fear. "This isn't funny."

"That's right. It isn't."

"You're scaring me."

"Christmas break starts this Friday, right?"

"No, Jack."

"Jill—listen! One more week and it's break time. Everyone heads for parts unknown. Except who? One Martin Rucker, that's who. Total geek-nerd loser that he is, Martin will be staying on campus. Poor guy has nowhere to go, you see. And my heart just bleeds for him."

"Jack—"

"It's lonely at Braddington. It's a lonely place, even when it's in session. But during winter break? Forget about it. Almost all the buildings are closed. Nobody around except a few alcoholic teachers with no family to go visit. And Martin, of course. I mean, seriously now, Jill, would you be surprised if over the course of a depressing Christmas break, old Martin was to do away with himself once and for all?"

Jack took his eyes off the winding two-lane black-top and glanced at Jill. She was staring at him, sober-faced, her eyes filled with disgust. He rushed on. "I know *I* would believe it, if Martin killed himself. I wouldn't question it for a second. Hey, the guy already tried to kill himself. The cops are going to be like—'Congratulations, Martin, this time you did it!'"

No response from Jill. Jack gritted his teeth.

"Okay. That's part one. Now here's where we start to get clever. Just in case—and I don't think this is likely, I really don't—but just in case the cops get suspicious and start thinking foul play? I've worked out the all-time perfect alibi for us, Jill. Get this. We're not even going to be here. At the time of Martin's death, we're going to be miles away."

He grinned at her, but she was looking down at her hands.

"You and me, Jill, are going to be on vacation. Blueberry Hill. It's a little vacation spot where my dad owns a ski chalet. It's a cozy little cabin, complete with a moose head over the fireplace. You'll love it. And it's perfect for what we need."

"Please stop."

"There are about twenty chalets on this big hill, all managed by this creepy old woman, Mrs. Dobb. She used to do a great business, too. But that was before Mount Rose shut down its slopes. Now when we go up there, there's no one around. As in, no witnesses? I figure, when we get there, I put in an appearance at Mrs. Dobb's main lodge, just so she can testify later that we were there.

"*But*, what she won't know—what no one is going to know—is that we're going to be bringing Martin along."

Jack noticed that he was gripping the wheel hard. His knuckles were white.

"But here's the best part of all. Hunt's mom lives only twenty minutes away from the chalet, over in Weston. And this weekend, Bradford, Cameron, Brooke, and Dede are all joining Hunt. Where? At his mom's. For a little snowmobile and toboggan action. So after we kill Martin—"

Jill gasped, and Jack had to stop talking for a moment to steady his voice. "After we kill Martin, we call Hunt. Just to get extra alibi material. Then we drive Martin back to town and dump him off the foot-bridge, so it looks like he jumped. Boom. Done. Over with. And then he's out of our lives, Jill, and nothing—nothing—can ever bother us again."

Jack took his hands off the wheel and made a wiping motion, to indicate how completely they'd be done with Martin. Then he gripped the wheel again as the car started to drift into the left lane—and a pair of onrushing headlights. Jill braced herself against the dash as he glided the car back into his lane.

"Then," he said, "the next morning? We invite Hunt and the gang over to the chalet. Just to cement the alibi even more. So that way, everyone can honestly say we were nowhere near school when Martin died."

Jack was finally done. He drove for a long while in silence. When the radio started playing the old Talking Heads song "Psycho Killer," he reached over and snapped it off. The Braddington Paper Mill loomed on the right. He went by as fast as he could. He knew Jill hated the sight of the place.

He was dying of tension waiting for Jill to say something. Like maybe she would whip out a badge and say, "Pull over, you're under arrest." Ever since Jack had started planning the murder, he'd felt intensely guilty, as if he'd already done it. Whenever he was alone—reading, walking, whatever—he had this horrible feeling like he was committing a crime.

"You're teasing me, right?" Jill asked finally. "This whole thing is like one big practical joke."

The anger suddenly surged through him. "You see another way out of this?"

She glared at him in the darkness of the car. "No," she said, "I don't. But you're talking murder. *Murder!*"

"So?"

"So? Helloo! Anybody home?"

"Look, Jill, it's not really murder."

"Oh no? What do you call it?"

"The guy's nuts. He's totally suicidal, am I right? That night at my dad's house when he—didn't he tell

119

you how he hated himself so much he wanted to kill himself?"

"That was just to get me to pity him."

"No, Jill it's true. He's suicidal. I'm telling you. He's going to kill himself someday. One way or another. We're just assisting him. It's a mercy killing."

"Right."

"You don't think he deserves to die? After what he did to you?"

"It was the worst night of my life," she said genuinely. "But Jack—it's still not something you kill people for. I mean, Jack, do you know how crazy you sound? I'm serious, it's like you and Martin have switched places or something."

"Jill, I'm telling you, I'm a smart guy. I've been over this and over it and over it. It's the only way. And I'll tell you something else. It's absolutely foolproof."

"That's what you said about sneaking into your room."

"Well this time it's—"

"No, Jack! No! And that's final! Don't bring it up ever again! I mean it!"

But that night, Jack was summoned to the pay phone in the common room.

"Guess what Martin wants?" Jill asked as soon as Jack said hello. He could hear the fury in her voice.

Jack pressed the receiver hard against his ear. "He called you?"

"He netted me on my computer. He wants you to sneak me into your dorm again, Jack."

"No!"

"Only this time, he wants you to sneak me into *his* room. It's just across the hall, he says. He says we can use the basement trick again. And again and again—he says he wants to make this a weekly ritual—or else he turns us in."

Jack slammed the pay phone hard with the heel of his hand. After the crashing ceased, Jill said, "Jack?"

"Yeah."

"I already netted him back. I told him yes, Jack."

Jack inhaled sharply.

"But I told him we'd have to start *after* Christmas break. I told him I had this wicked bad cold. Do you know why I told him that, Jack?" There was a tremble in her voice now.

"Jill," he told her in a whisper. "It's the only way. Trust me!"

He glanced around for the umpteenth time, making sure he was still alone in the common room; then he lowered his voice still further.

"Jill, I'm not crazy, right? If I didn't know this was going to work, I'd never suggest it. You know that, don't you? So are we agreed on the, uh, plan?"

Jill was silent. But Jack felt a wave of relief.

He knew what her silence meant.

The murder was on.

CHAPTER 17

ON FRIDAY AFTERNOON AT EXACTLY FOUR o'clock, there was a gigantic scream from the Braddington campus. Kids all over the school had their heads out their windows, shouting their lungs out.

It was the traditional way the students celebrated the end of semester. It was one of the few acts of bad behavior that the faculty condoned. Then again, what choice did they have? They couldn't kick out the entire school at once.

That night, the first night of Braddington's three-week winter break, it started to snow. Thick fat flakes fell gently, fluttering down from a black sky. Such a pretty night.

Whitman Hall was practically empty. So there was no one around to hear the nursery rhymes playing softly in room 3-H. No one to hear the soft whimpering.

No one around except Jack.

He knocked on the door. And again.

The whimpering stopped. Then there was a rustling sound. And a moment later the light behind the peephole went dark. Martin was looking out. Just the way he had on that fateful Monday afternoon. Jack forced himself to smile at the door.

The door opened.

Martin's peanut face was even paler than usual. And tearstained.

"Hey, buddy," Jack said, smiling warmly.

Martin sniffed. Behind him was the trash heap of junk that was his room. In the corner, next to Martin's computer terminal, sat the old record player in its tan case, the worn Uncle Phil record album propped up beside it. Uncle Phil, a bald guy with a huge round face, grinned out at Jack like the man in the moon. The musty, cheesy smell of year-old socks curled its way into Jack's nose. He tried to breathe through his mouth.

"I thought you . . . had gone," Martin said, wiping at his eyes with the sleeve of his greasy suit.

"Without *you*?"

"Your suitcase was gone again. And I couldn't find your car."

Jack waggled a finger. "Did you go in my room again?"

Martin looked so worn-out and weepy that Jack almost felt sorry for him, especially considering what was about to happen to him. Good-bye, Martin.

"So listen," Jack said. "Jill and I are going on a little weekend getaway. We wanted to know if you wanted to come along."

Martin's eyes widened with disbelief. "You're *inviting* me?"

"Of course."

Jack could see the doubt flicker in those big baby eyes. He kept his grin steady. "Look, Martin," he said. "I'll be honest. You've got us where you want us. What can we do? We've decided we're not going to fight it anymore. We're going to do this your way.

We want you along so we don't have to worry, you know, about what you'll do."

"That's very wise, Jack."

"Thank you."

Martin glanced down the dark hallway. "Is this a trick?" he asked suddenly.

Jack's left eye started twitching. "You are so paranoid, Martin, really, it's unbelievable. No, it's not a trick. We want you to come with us. Otherwise, you'll go right to Simmons. We know that."

"Simmons is gone."

"So you'll go to Dean Schmidt."

"That's right. I was going to, Jack." Martin grinned at the memory. "But first, you know what I was going to do? I was going to tell your dad! See?" He held up a little piece of paper, where he'd scribbled the number. "I even went so far as to get the number from information."

Stay calm, Jack told himself. It was just one more reason that they had to do what they were going to do.

"Well, well," said Jack, "I'm glad I knocked when I did."

Martin laughed. But then he looked sad again.

"Look," Jack said. "I know you won't believe this, but we've gotten used to spending time with you. I don't think it would be the same without you there. In fact, I know it wouldn't."

Martin giggled. "I'm a lot of fun, really. Most guys don't know that about me."

"You know what I always say, Martin. You don't let them know. Now come on. Get packed."

Martin turned and stared blankly at his trash-filled room. "Packed?" he wondered vaguely.

"Where are your new clothes? Bring them."

"Well, I—"

"Throw some stuff in a suitcase. I've got to run a few errands in town, then I've got to pick up Jill. We'll be waiting for you over by Crest Hollow."

Crest Hollow was a dark deserted street that ran along the back of the campus.

"Well, can you wait just a second?" Martin asked. "I could use some help packing, as a matter of fact. Then I could help you run your errands and we could pick Jill up together."

And risk someone seeing you with me? thought Jack. No way, José. He clapped a hand down on Martin's shoulder. The guy had the frail bones of a bird. "You're afraid we're going to leave without you, aren't you? You're forgetting again. You won."

"Oh, that's very nice of you to say, Jack, but I mean"—he wiped his face nervously—"I don't know exactly what to take. And—where are we going anyway?"

There was fear in his face. And even though Jack knew that it was his job to calm Martin down, he was glad to see the terror. Glad, glad, glad.

"Skiing," Jack said, raising and lowering his eyebrows to make the idea seem as exciting as possible. "We're going skiing."

Martin's mouth dropped open with a tiny gasp. He covered it with both hands. Then he clutched his hair like a game show contestant who has just hit the jackpot. "Oh, my goodness! Oh, my goodness! This is so great!"

But then his eyes narrowed. "Waaaait a minute!"
Jack shivered.

"Jill told me she has this wicked cold," Martin said.

"She does. Or did. She's actually feeling much better. But she'll probably hang around the chalet while you and I have all the fun. C'mon, Martin—what do I have to do? Beg? I thought you'd jump at the idea."

The doubt cleared out of Martin's face again, like a passing cloud. He began to jump up and down, chanting, "Skiing, skiing, we're going skiing." Jack was afraid the weirdo would try to give him a hug and a kiss.

"Okay," Jack said. "Easy, big fella. Now hurry up and pack and meet us in . . ." He checked his watch. "Can you make it in about ten minutes?"

"Of course, Jack," Martin promised. "Of course."

Martin stayed at his door, watching Jack head off down the dark hallway to the stairs, as if he still didn't believe his good fortune.

"He's coming," Jack told Jill when he got in the car.

"Jack, I haven't agreed to this. You know that, don't you?"

It was a lie. She had agreed about a hundred times, it was just that she'd also backed out a hundred times.

"Just go with me to Blueberry Hill, that's all I'm asking," he lied right back.

"And you're not going to do anything?"

"Not unless I get your permission," Jack promised.

They sat in silence.

"Should we go over the plan again?" Jack asked.

"Why?" Jill said, giving him a frantic look. "You just said we're not doing it."

"Just in case we do do it."

"But we're not!"

Jack shrugged, tapping the dash with his black gloved fingers.

"Where is he?" Jill said, peering through the windshield up the snow-covered slope that led to the tall metal fence that circled the campus.

"He'll be here any minute," Jack promised.

"What's he doing?"

"He's probably trying to borrow a crane so he can haul away some of his junk and find a clean piece of underwear. He'll be here. Just relax."

But it was twenty more minutes before Martin finally tromped through the snow toward them. He was lugging an old-fashioned brown suitcase that was obviously well traveled.

Apparently Martin was feeling festive. He had put on a straw hat. He pressed his bulbous nose against the glass of Jill's window, eyeing her like a zombie. Jill powered down her window. "Hey," she said cheerfully. "The Martin Man."

There were snowflakes in his eyes, as if he were wearing white mascara. "My sweetest, most gorgeous prize," he murmured. He reached into the car and found Jill's hand, pulling it toward the window, where he kissed it. "Should you be out like this, my princess, with your cold the way it is?"

"It's a lot better," Jill told him. "Thanks."

"I told you," Jack reminded him. "C'mon, buddy, hop in."

Like an extra passenger, a musty smell entered the car along with Martin, the odor quickly winning out over the luscious dark smell of the car's leather seats. Just as Martin was about to sit down, though, he backed out of the car all over again. He looked up on the roof, then stared down at Jack with surprise. "Where are the skis?"

"The what?" Jack asked stupidly. "Oh, the skis, yeah. We're, uh, going to rent them at the slopes, big guy."

Martin looked unsure, but he smiled. "Goody," he said. He got back into the car.

Jack smiled at Jill, who was giving him a half smile back. There was fury in her eyes that said, "What have you got me into this time?"

Only Murder One, he felt like answering her.

127

ERIC WEINER

As he pulled out onto Crest Hollow he was vaguely aware of the dark blue Chevy drifting along behind him. Funny. The car didn't have its lights on.

He stepped on the gas.

CHAPTER 18

"JACK AND JILL WENT UP THE HILL," SANG Jack, "to fetch a pail of waterrrr—"

"Jack," Jill said with a warning in her voice.

"What?"

"Stop it."

"You hate my singing? She hates my singing, Martin," Jack said to the rearview mirror.

Martin was slouched against the side window, staring out silently. Around the time they'd passed the "Now Entering Vermont" sign, Martin had fallen into a very sullen mood.

"You're awful quiet back there," Jack said. "You okay?"

"I'm having a sad thought," Martin said.

"Well, no sad thoughts, pal. This is vacation."

Jill gave him another angry look, then she swiveled in her seat. "Tell me," she said to Martin.

What was all this concern Jill was feeling for Martin all of a sudden? Jack thought angrily. As if the guy hadn't been blackmailing and torturing them for the past month.

But he knew what it was. They were going to kill

Martin in less than an hour. She was feeling sorry for the poor slob. It was only natural.

"When I was nine, my mother took me on vacation to Switzerland," Martin said, still looking out the window. "She said she was going to teach me how to ski. I was so excited, I thought I was going to die. I hadn't seen Mother in over a year, you see. I had almost given up hope. But it turned out . . ."

There was a long silence from the backseat. Jill gave Jack a meaningful look; he rolled his eyes.

"It turned out," Martin went on, his voice getting all crumbly, "that she was meeting her new lover there for a secret tryst. It wasn't enough that she had left my father for another man. But now she was cheating on the new man as well."

Jack flicked on the radio—loud.

"Jack," Jill said.

He flicked it back off.

"What's the matter with you?" she asked him.

"They went skiing *every day,*" Martin went on, lost in his reverie. "They left me in the hotel. I was so miserable that finally one day I drank a whole glass of kitchen cleanser mixed with milk. I had to be taken to the hospital to have my stomach pumped. Mother said I had ruined her vacation and promised me she would never take me anywhere with her ever again. She was true to her word, too."

There were tears all over Martin's face now, though Jack hadn't heard him crying. Then he saw the tear roll down Jill's cheek. That stung.

"Well, don't worry, Martin," Jack told him. "This vacation you're going to have a ball. Believe me, it's going to wipe out that memory once and for all."

And right then—right in the middle of everything— guilt smacked him hard in the chest, like a shotgun blast ripping a hole through his heart.

What were they doing?

The road they were driving on was lined with signs and billboards announcing various ski hotel packages. Then came the large green sign, EXIT 29. "Almost there," Jack said.

His announcement was greeted with silence. There was a terrible tension beginning to build in the car.

To get to Blueberry Hill, you had to leave the paved roads for dirt ones, and drive through a tiny downtown with the standard Vermont country store (for the tourists, of course; no native Vermonters shopped there). Then a few more turns and the hill itself loomed on the right. A sign with a carved wooden hand pointed out the direction.

BLUEBERRY HILL

"You know, Martin, Jill—we've got to come back here sometime this summer. The hill was mainly designed for snow bunnies, but it's in the summer that you see why it got its name. Blueberries—big as bumblebees."

Feeling like the most loathsome creature alive, Jack started up the road that wound around the hill. There were more wooden signs now, with wooden hands pointing out the directions, left for chalets 1–10 and right for 11–20 and straight ahead for the lodge. He went straight.

The dirt road was frozen solid. They drove at a steep angle, through the thick masses of green pines and white birches on either side. The fresh piney smell of the woods was seeping into the car.

When he saw the lodge up ahead, he started to slow down. He didn't want to park too far away, or Martin would get suspicious. But he didn't want to park too close, or Mrs. Dobb might see him.

"Road looks icy," he muttered, pulling over to the

side. "Wait here, guys, I just have to let Mrs. Dobb know we're here."

He slammed the door shut without looking back and scrambled up the path toward the big log-cabin-style building whose hanging sign said DOBB'S LODGE.

The air was so cold he could feel the hairs inside his nose freezing, and when he breathed in, his nostrils stuck together. The snow underfoot was crunching and squeaking. When he reached the lodge's front door, he glanced back at the car. Martin was giving him a worried look. Jack waved.

It's the only way, he told himself, pleading with his conscience.

Then he went in.

The front of the lodge was a big living room with a huge arching stone fireplace and rough-hewn furniture, all made from shellacked slabs of wood. Ahead was the staircase that led up to Mrs. Dobb's private quarters. Down the hall were the guest room and the playroom, the dining room and the kitchen. To the right was the half door to Mrs. Dobb's office. Old Mrs. Dobb was sitting in there at her computer. She looked up in surprise.

"Oh, Jack," she said, taking off her reading glasses, "hello." She got up and waddled toward him. She was a short, overweight woman with a mass of straggly white hair. It looked as if it had snowed on her head and never melted. "So nice of you to stop by."

She put her cheek out for a kiss and Jack obliged her. "How are you?" she said, sneaking a peek past him out the window. She was such a nosy old biddy. He took one step to the side to block her view.

"You look . . . I don't know," she said. "Rough trip?"

"Not bad."

Her little eyes were piercing into him. Jack had to

remind himself that he hadn't killed Martin yet—the way she was studying him, he felt as if he were already covered with blood.

"So, did your father come with you after all?" she asked.

When Jack had called to say he'd be coming, he'd told her his father was probably going to show. "Nah," he said. "You know my dad. Mr. Reliable."

"Jack," Mrs. Dobb said, eyeing him suspiciously. "You didn't even tell your father you were coming, did you?"

Maybe he *was* bleeding. Was he suddenly sweating or was that snow melting on his neck and down his shirt?

"Have you got a girl in the car?" Mrs. Dobb asked. "You have, haven't you!" Giggling, she started to push past him.

"No, no, it's just me—" Jack said. His first impulse was to grab her. He resisted it. "Oh, all right," he said with a big grin. "You got me. She's in the car."

Mrs. Dobb turned back from the door and pulled at his arm, smiling conspiratorially. "Oh, now, Jack!" She chuckled. "You naughty boy."

"You won't tell on me, will you?"

More chuckling. Mrs. Dobb poked his chest. "Oh, now."

The old crone was actually flirting with him. "You know I won't tell, Jack." She pinched his cheek. "Oh, wouldn't it be nice to be a young thing like you again. Instead of rotting to death all by my lonesome, which is what I'm doing up here, I tell you. You know there are ten chalets empty this season?"

Jack was wild to get back to the car. He barely heard what she was saying. He nodded.

"I'm going to have to shut down pretty soon. And then where will I be?"

133

She was smiling, so Jack smiled back, as if what she was saying were funny. He patted her shoulder. "It'll be okay, I promise. Everything's going to work out just perfectly." He started back out the door. "We'll stop by tomorrow. I want you to meet her. She's really something, Mrs. Dobb."

"I'll bet she is, to snare a prize like you, Jack. I'll bet she is."

"All set," Jack told them when he got back in the car. "And now we can—"

He stopped short. Martin was resting his head in between the front bucket seats, and Jill was gently stroking his thin brown hair. Jill met Jack's amazed stare. Her eyes told him not to say a word. He was furious. But he obeyed.

Chalet 19, just like Chalets 1 to 18 as well as Chalet 20, was an A-frame with a wooden porch that jutted out from the side, like an A+. The way the Washburns' chalet was placed—nestled into the side of the icy slope—the porch jutted out over a ten-foot drop. Not a big enough drop, Martin my boy, thought Jack as he pulled the luggage out of the trunk.

Farther up the steep, steep hill perched the next and last A-frame, Chalet 20. Even though the chalet was far away, Jack was relieved to see that its windows were dark.

As Martin emerged from the car he looked like a little boy wrapped in a blanket. His long topcoat stretched down to the ground, forcing him to hold up the hem as he walked. It made him look pathetic, which wasn't the effect Jack wanted him to be having on Jill right now.

"Maybe we can roast marshmallows," Jill was telling him. "Would you like that?"

Yes, Mommy, thought Jack, I would.

And now he was sure it was sweat he was feeling, not snow.

"Jill," Jack said. "Give me a hand here, will ya?"

Martin didn't offer to help, he noticed, as always.

When Jill came back around the trunk of the car, he hissed, "What are you being so nice to him for?"

She glared at him.

"As soon as we get inside," he told her.

"No," she breathed.

He slammed the trunk.

Martin was standing on the porch, looking forlorn and worried.

"Don't expect too much, guys," Jack called gaily. "My father may be a multimillionaire, but he's also a tightwad." Jack found the key and turned it in the lock, pushing the door open wide enough for Jill and Martin to go in ahead of him.

Jack had told the truth. The chalet was nothing much. Upstairs there were three bedrooms with bunk beds—for big ski parties. The living room had a stone fireplace, a baby version of the one in Mrs. Dobb's main lodge. The whole place was carpeted with this thin blue AstroTurf-like stuff. It was supposed to be able to handle all the snow and trampling it endured, but it always smelled a little mildewy. Other than a few pieces of slab-wood furniture, the only unusual decoration was the moose head with its big sharp antlers, mounted on the wall over the fireplace. It stared straight ahead with huge dark eyes.

"It's very cozy," Martin said politely. His teeth were chattering and his lips were blue.

"Here," Jack said, marching Martin to the wing chair. "We're going to get you warmed up, buster." He pulled the chair up close to the fireplace and

135

pushed Martin down into it. "I'll get the fire started right away. Jill, you want to get some cocoa going?"

Jill was just standing there, staring at them. She had unsnapped her green overcoat and untied her scarf, and Jack could see her black sweater slowly rising and falling as she breathed hard.

"Jill? Cocoa?"

"R-right."

"You want to see what a cheapskate my dad is?" Jack said to Martin. "Look at this." He pulled on one of the large hearthstones near the fireplace's base. The rock came loose. Jack set it on the stone floor in front of the fireplace. "It's been like this for years. He's never paid to get it fixed."

He glanced at Jill, who was still standing in the middle of the room, frozen, staring at him. He glared at her. She headed for the kitchenette.

There was a stack of wood next to the fireplace. Jack pulled back the fire screen, threw some logs on the metal stand, then crumpled up balls of old yellow newspaper from the pile by the wall. He took the large box of matches off the stone mantel, struck one, and held it against the paper until the heat began to singe the tiny hairs on his hand. Then he picked up the long iron poker.

"You really seem to know what you're doing, Jack," Martin said. He gulped when Jack turned toward him, the spearlike poker grasped in his hand.

"What? Oh, yeah, thanks. Well, there's nothing much to starting a fire. I'll teach you on the next one, whaddaya say?"

"Jack?" Jill called from the kitchen area. She had all the cupboards open. "I don't see any cocoa."

"Oh," Jack said. Still holding the poker, he pretended to think for a moment. "Oh, yeah. You know where there's some cocoa? In the upstairs closet."

"In the upstairs closet?" Martin asked. He was really looking scared now. He knows! He knows! Jack thought wildly. It was actually a thrilling thought, in a way. It made the whole plan more real.

"We rent the place out sometimes," Jack explained, "so my miser father locks everything upstairs so the renters won't be able to use any of his precious stuff."

Jill started up the stairs. Martin darted a glance from Jill back to Jack. "But if it's locked," Martin said, starting to rise, "how can she get in?"

Jack put a hand on Martin's shoulder, holding him down. "What are you so jumpy about? You're on vacation, Martin. You can relax now."

"But—"

"Everything's unlocked, because we haven't had any renters in months. This whole place, Blueberry Hill? It's dying, man."

The fire was blazing now. Jack jabbed at the logs with his poker, turning them over and sending up showers of sparks. He could feel the heat baking his dungarees. It felt good.

"Feel that heat, Martin?" Jack asked.

Martin nodded, or was he just shivering?

"And in just a second Jill's going to make you some yummy yummy cocoa and warm up your tummy."

"That sounds . . . very good, Jack," said Martin miserably. He was shaking more violently now.

"Jack?" Jill called from upstairs. "I can't find it— the cocoa."

Jack froze. He could feel Martin staring at him. "Try the drawer in the table next to the bed in the master bedroom."

"The drawer in the table . . ." Martin repeated. He licked his lips. "Jack . . . what's going on?"

Now the sweat was running down Jack's forehead and stinging his eyes. He smiled at Martin.

"Don't you know?"

"No, no, I don't know."

Martin started to get up again, but Jack pressed the spear tip of the poker against his chest. He leaned forward, leering into Martin's face. "We're making you something hot to drink," he said. Then he laughed. He was almost hysterical.

"You k-know what?" Martin said. He was getting up now, and Jack let him. But as Martin moved right Jack took a step to his left so he could keep Martin from getting to the door if he tried to bolt.

"I-I think I'm going to go for a little walk," Martin said.

"A little walk? *Now?*"

"You and Jill," Martin said. "You probably want to be alone for a little while. It was nice enough of you to let me come along on this trip. But you need some privacy. Even I know that."

"But, Martin, we love your company," Jack said.

Martin still looked cold, but he was sweating, too, now.

"Jack?"

Both their heads jerked toward the sound. Jill was coming down the stairs. She was holding a gun.

Martin's hands started working in the air, wriggling like worms. "Oh, God, Oh, God . . ."

Jill's hand was shaking, too, as she came down the stairs into the living room. She stopped at the base of the stairs, pointing the gun at Martin.

Martin swiveled his head frantically back and forth between Jack and Jill. Then, abruptly, he started to laugh.

"Oh, now, very very funny," he said. He clutched his chest. "Oh, you did have me going there for a

138

moment. Oh, my my my. *Très amusant!* But you can't scare me, my friends. I know you'd never do anything that stupid—ha-ha."

He turned his back on Jill, crossing to the sofa, flopping down. He put his feet up. "As if you'd kill me. Really now. What would be the point? I've only got till graduation, anyway. After that, I know you won't want to be my friends. Believe me, I have no illusions. But if you shoot me, then it's jail for life—or worse."

He was talking his usual flippant talk, but Jack could tell he was scared, too. And not just because he was still shaking. His face was white as paper.

And then—

Jack raised the poker over his head and brought it down with all his might.

Only inches from Martin's head.

Martin screamed. "Come on now, Jack!" he said with terror and with anger, too. "Is that really fun, to torture me like this?"

"You tell *me!*" Jack yelled, and on the final word he brought the poker down again, this time at Martin's feet. Martin pulled his feet back, but Jack was aiming carefully. He wasn't going to hit him. Not yet.

"Jack, stop it."

Jill said it quietly, but in a tone that made them both look up. She still had the gun, but she was pointing it at Jack now. "Put down the poker," she ordered.

Jack laughed.

She jabbed the gun at him. "I mean it! Put it down!"

Jack took two giant steps over to the fireplace and dropped the poker back into the metal tool bucket. He held up both hands, to show he was weaponless.

139

Martin was gulping hard. "You guys are serious, aren't you?"

"Congratulations," Jack said. "You finally caught on."

"Good God! Are you insane?"

"No," Jack said, "that's your department."

Springing forward like a cat, he grabbed Martin roughly, pulling him up. Martin went all limp, like a rag doll. Jack turned him around so he was facing Jill. Jill was screaming for him to let Martin go.

Jack did as he was told. He backed away from Martin. "Now shoot him," he told Jill. "Shoot him, the way we said!"

Jill was crying. So was Martin.

"I didn't mean any harm," Martin said. "I swear. I just wanted to be your friend."

"Too late for that, Martin," Jack said, stepping slowly back toward the fireplace. "You've been torturing us, little fella. Now you get to feel what it's like."

Martin cried harder. His little shoulders shook. "I'm so sorry. I really really am. I won't do it ever again. I promise. So help me."

"That's one promise you're going to keep, Martin."

"Oh, *please*!" Martin raised his hands to him, begging. "You don't know what it's like . . . I mean . . . when I saw you together . . . that day? . . . in your room? I listened at the door, Jack. It was so beautiful, the two of you . . . so happy. . . ."

"Shoot him, Jill."

Jill cocked the trigger. She was aiming at Jack again, but the sound did the trick anyway. It was just like Jack had planned. The clicking of the trigger got Martin to turn around.

Then he started sobbing. He bowed his head, blubbering like a baby. "I—I love you both . . . so much . . . I just wanted . . . to be your friend."

140

Jill screamed, *"Jack!"*

But it was too late. Jack had stepped up behind Martin, and now he brought the loose rock from the fireplace down on Martin's head.

Jack had always been a natural athlete. Once, at a carnival, he'd won a large stuffed animal for a date by swinging the big wooden hammer so hard he rang the bell. Now he brought the rock down just as hard, and landed it right where he wanted it, too, flush in the back of Martin's brown head.

The rock made a thud so satisfying Jack wouldn't have been surprised to see Martin's head disappear down into his neck. And when he pulled the rock back, a mass of blood and clotted gray gunk came with it.

Jill was still screaming as Martin stumbled forward. He took two steps, hands in the air, then fell, face-first, down onto the white sofa, like a little boy about to have a good long cry.

He stayed in that position, awfully still, as his blood dripped down onto the sofa and the floor.

Jill dropped the gun and covered her face. She was sobbing as hard as Martin just had.

And then the phone started to ring.

CHAPTER 19

JACK STARED AT THE BLACK OLD-FASHIONED rotary dial that sat on the wooden dining table by the kitchenette. The ringing sounded incredibly loud—almost like a scream.

Jack's instincts were all shouting, Don't answer! But that was wrong, wrong! Because the whole plan was based on their alibi. *They were supposed to be here.*

Jill was crying. No help there. He set the bloody rock down on the floor, then crossed to the phone, making a wide circle around Martin's dead body.

"Hello?"

"Hey, Jack."

"Who's this?"

"Who's this? Wow, Jack, you really know how to put school out of your mind when you go off for break, now don't you?"

"Hunt?"

"No fooling, Sherlock."

Jack just stood there, holding the phone, forgetting to talk.

"Jack, are you stoned or something? You sound brain-dead."

"No, no, no, I'm just . . ."

"Just what? Ohhhhhh, I get it. You and Jill, huh?"

"Me and Jill what?"

"I caught you, didn't I?"

"Caught us? What are you talking about!"

"Now, don't get so upset, Jack. So I caught you at kind of a delicate moment, huh, big guy?"

You caught us, all right, Jack was thinking. Jill was moving toward the sofa. Jack waved his free hand in the air, signaling her to stay away.

"Hey," Hunt said. "You guys must be jumping for joy to finally be getting a break from Dr. Creepo, huh?"

"Who?"

"Jack, are you drunk or something? Seriously. You can tell old Hunt."

"No, I—"

"Serves Rucker right, though, doesn't it?"

"What does?"

"You know, having to stay all by himself in Whitman. Whoa—wait a minute. He didn't find out where you are, did he? That's it, isn't it? That's why you sound so strange. He's there with you right now."

"No! What are you talking about?"

"Oh, good. You scared me there for a second. Hey, Jack, maybe he'll kill himself over break, did you ever think about that? I'm sure you did, you sly dog, you."

"Hunt, now's not the best time for me to—"

"I got you, I got you. Okay, I'll cut to the chase. Guess what my idiot mother forgot to tell me? Both snowmobiles are in the shop. Engines are shot."

Jack was only vaguely listening. He watched Jill sit down in the chair across from Martin's body. She was crying silently now, rocking back and forth.

". . . so we'll be there in about fifteen, twenty minutes, okay, Captain?"

143

Jack suddenly realized what Hunt was saying. The words snapped him back to attention.

"You'll *what?*"

"We're bored out of our minds, man. We're coming over."

"No! I mean—Hunt, seriously, that is not a good idea."

"It's a great idea, are you kidding?"

Jill had slowly uncovered her face. Her cheeks were wet with tears, her eyes red and blurry, but those eyes were fixed on Jack now, studying him with a new horror.

"Hunt," Jack said, "you know what? You were right before . . . about Jill and me needing some time alone—"

"You've got the whole break ahead of you," Hunt said sourly. "Don't be selfish." He started to whisper. "Dede's been whining, all about how I never pay attention to her. I feel like killing her. I never should have brought her up here, Captain. I don't know what I was thinking of. Except for that luscious bod of hers." He cackled. "Anyway, we'll be right over."

"Hunt! No! Hunt? Hello?"

But the line had gone dead.

CHAPTER 20

JILL WAS ON HER FEET. "WHAT?" SHE whispered.

"They're coming."

"Who's coming?"

"They're all coming. Hunt, Cameron, everybody."

Jack was pacing up and down, clutching his head.

"Here?!" Jill cried.

"Yeah, here, what do you think?"

"Don't shout at me!"

"I'm not shouting at you!"

"You are!"

"All right, so I'm shouting at you, I'm just a little tense, that's all. Okay?"

He stared at his watch. Ten of nine. "Okay," he said. "It's okay." He tried to think. "We're just going to have to move fast."

"Move fast?"

"Clean up," Jack said. He forced himself to head for Martin's body. He bent down and scooped up the corpse in his arms. For a little kid, Martin's dead body felt incredibly heavy. His head lolled, his eyes opening like a doll's when you tilt the head back. There was a dark red circle of blood on the white sofa and another large puddle on the floor. "I'm going to take him down to the basement. You start cleaning up the blood."

He was halfway to the basement door when Jill screamed. He turned so fast he bashed Martin's head against the door frame, splattering more blood, more blood that would have to cleaned up—and cleaned up *now*.

Jill was standing by the kitchen sink, her hands up near her face, her mouth open.

"What?" Jack hissed.

"The water!"

"What about it?"

"There's no water."

"What are you talking about?!"

"Jack!"

She gestured vaguely toward the sink as Jack finally realized what she was talking about. His father must have turned the water off so the pipes wouldn't freeze.

Jack swore. Then he turned back and started down the basement steps with Martin's body.

"Jack—where are you—"

His arms were aching. He staggered across the tiny dusty cobwebbed basement to the large white freezer. His mother had used the freezer to store loads of frozen meat for their big ski parties, back when his parents' marriage had still been a happy one, and they still had lots of friends.

Jack didn't make it. He dropped Martin three feet before he got to the freezer. Splattering more blood.

"Jack?"

It was Jill at the top of the stairs. She was crying again. "What are we going to do?"

Jack didn't even bother to answer her. He didn't

want to waste time. He flipped up the freezer's heavy coffinlike lid, breathing a sigh of relief when he saw that the freezer was practically empty. He dumped Martin inside, then slammed the lid shut.

"Jaaaack," Jill said tearfully. "They're coming!"

"I know they're coming."

Jack started dodging around the basement. "Help me!" he shouted.

"Help you what?"

"Help me find the spigot that turns the water back on!"

Jill came partway down the stairs. "It's down here?"

"I don't know! I guess so."

"Maybe it's outside somewhere."

Jack was hunting desperately around the boiler. He didn't see any knobs or spigots that looked promising. He did find a large metal pail, however.

"What's that for?" Jill asked him as he charged toward her. Then she shrieked so piercingly that he froze in his tracks.

"What?!"

"Your feet. You're tracking—"

He looked down, then whirled—

You could follow the trail he had made as he ran around the basement—a trail of bloody boot prints.

He charged up the steps. No time to worry about that now.

Jill followed him back into the living room. "Where are you going?"

"To get water."

Jill started after him.

"Stay here," he ordered her.

"Why? Jack, don't leave me," she whimpered. "With the body. I-I can't—"

"Okay! Come on."

147

Neither of them was wearing a coat as they clattered down the steps of the back porch. Jack started climbing the snowy hill toward their neighbor's dark chalet. Jill followed him.

The air was freezing, working its way through every patch of Jack's bare skin. Good, he thought vaguely. If he froze to death, all his problems would be solved.

Chalet 20 was dark. Maybe there was nobody home.

The back door was locked. Jack cursed foully.

"The porch!" Jill suggested.

Getting up on the porch was a problem in itself. But by approaching the porch from the side, they were able to swing themselves up and over the crosshatched wooden railing. Jack clasped the white metal handle of the sliding door with frozen fingers. He pulled.

The glass door glided open.

Yes!

They went in.

They found themselves in a living room whose layout was almost identical to the Washburn chalet, even down to the placement of the furniture. There was a different brand of furniture, and different pictures on the mantel, but otherwise it looked the same. Except there was no moose over the fireplace. And no dead body.

The two teenagers stood on the thin blue carpet, just inside the porch, listening hard. Suddenly Jill grabbed Jack's arm.

He turned to her in alarm.

But she shook her head to show that she hadn't heard anything. "Jack," she whispered. "Look at you."

There was no way he could see himself, but he could tell by her expression how bad he looked.

148

"You're covered with blood," she told him. "Don't touch a thing. Here."

With her clean hand, she took the pail from him, careful not to touch where he had held the metal handle. The handle, Jack saw, was wet with blood. Jill tiptoed across the living room to the kitchenette, tilting the pail so it fit under the sink's faucet. Hesitantly, she reached for the cold water tap. She turned it. There was a reassuring gush of water.

She turned to Jack, her face flooded with relief.

He grinned back at her.

The water drummed into the bottom of the pail, and then grew quieter as the pail began to fill. Jack watched as she carefully washed the blood off the rim of the pail and off her right hand. Good girl. Very thorough. Then, when the pail was full, she lugged it—slopping some onto the rug—back across the living room with two hands.

Jack held out his hands to take it from her. "We should have brought two pails," he muttered.

"This'll be enough," she whispered back. She set the pail down with a bang on the low wooden coffee table.

Then they heard the voices.

They were coming up the front porch. . . .

CHAPTER 21

THE MAN CAME IN FIRST. HE WAS A CRAGGY-faced man in his mid-thirties, wearing a black knit ski cap and a thick wool overcoat with wooden buckles. His bushy mustache seemed to cover his entire mouth. "You don't understand," he was saying angrily. "*You* don't have to worry. You just leave the whole money question up to—"

He stopped, staring down at the wet patches on the carpet. He knelt down, feeling the wet spots. Then he stared across the room at the sliding door.

Jack, who was standing behind the curtains to the right of the porch door, mouthed a curse.

Jill had left the porch door slightly open. She had also left the pail, bolting like a stag when she heard the people coming. Jack had crossed back to the coffee table to get the water, which didn't give him enough time to make it outside.

The man strode across the room and stood at the door, staring out into the darkness. He was maybe two feet away.

The man had left the chalet's front door open. A tall blond-haired woman in a pink parka and white

150

turtleneck came in, stomping her boots on the mat inside. She shut the door behind her and locked it. "I do understand, David," she said. "I understand perfectly, that's what you never understand."

David didn't answer.

The woman headed straight for the kitchenette. She glanced in the sink. "The faucet must be dripping," she said idly. "Tell Dobb."

Then she crossed to the fridge and pulled out something, Jack couldn't see what. "You know what we need?" she said with a sigh. "Wine."

"None for me."

"Well, *I'm* having."

Jack heard the twisting of a corkscrew.

"All I'm saying is," the woman went on, "I know you're going to find another job. I mean you . . . always"—*pop!* the cork came out—"do."

"Not with the computer industry the way it is right now."

The man shut the porch door the remaining inch. Then he moved away from the door at last. He stood at the coffee table with his hands in his pockets. Then he angrily riffled through one of the magazines that was lying there. And then—he traced his finger in a circle on the table's wooden surface, right where Jill had put the pail. He looked back at the porch door.

"It'll get better," the woman said.

"So you say."

"So I say. And in the meantime money is a little tight for us. So what?"

"Very tight."

"Very tight. Whatever. We've been in tight spots before, David. I mean, if you could just relax a little bit and stop obsessing about money, money, money, then this could be a real vacation for us." Her tone

151

changed, softened. "David, let's drink this upstairs, what do you say?"

Say yes, Jack silently prayed. Say yes. He thought his heart was going to burst. He could feel it expanding in his chest with each beat.

"All right," the man said finally.

And then he looked up, right where Jack was hiding. His eyes met Jack's.

"Come on," the woman said.

"Coming," the man grumbled.

And then he turned away. Jack couldn't imagine how the man had missed him—but he must have because—

Jack heard a set of light footsteps on the stairs. Then the man's heavy steps, following her.

"Easy! Watch it! Careful!" Jill ordered Jack as they crashed down through the woods back toward their chalet. Then Jack stopped, bracing his body against the peeling bark of a tall white birch.

"What took you so long? I was dying out here," Jill whispered.

"Well, I was dying in there, believe me."

"Did they see you?"

"No."

"How?"

"Never mind!" He looked down the hill. In their haste, they hadn't run back down from the chalet the same way they had run up. And now Jack was looking at a treacherous patch of icy slope. "Here, hold this a sec," he told Jill, handing her the pail.

"Careful—*Jack!*"

As Jack took his first step down—reaching out with his bare hand for a birch branch to steady himself—his foot shot out from under him. And the next

152

thing he knew he was tumbling down the ice like a ball.

It was a short fall, because he smacked his head hard against a rock. His forehead burned with pain.

"Are you okay?" Jill was peering down at him through the darkness.

"Yeah, fine," Jack told her. He stood up, feeling a little woozy and unsteady on his feet. "Hand me the bucket."

Jill gasped. "Jack, your head."

Jack felt his forehead. It stung badly. He pulled his hands away at once. They were sticky with fresh blood, his own this time.

"You've got this wicked cut—"

"Just hand me the bucket!" he snapped.

She handed down the bucket. He took it and set it down hard in the snow. Then he reached up for her, but she was too far away. "Slide down on your butt," he advised her.

But Jill had already taken a step down—

And now she was tumbling after him.

Jack was able to catch her, but ended up getting smacked back against another tree and getting the wind knocked out of him. Worse, his boot kicked the pail, sloshing away another inch of precious water.

When they finally made it back inside their chalet, there was only half a pail left.

And who knew how many minutes or seconds they had left before their guests arrived.

CHAPTER 22

TEN MINUTES LATER HUNT'S BMW CRUNCHED up the frozen snow of the drive outside the chalet. Jack saw the headlights filtering through the birch trees.

"They're here," he said hollowly.

He was standing in the middle of the living room, pressing a blue dish towel hard against the gash in his forehead. He was sweating hard from all the running around they'd just done. He turned to survey the room as best he could with his hand and the towel obscuring his view. It looked completely ordinary, just as it had looked when they first arrived. No body. No blood. The loose stone was back in the fireplace. It was as if Martin Rucker had never existed.

"We're fine," he said.

He caught a glimpse of Jill; her face had a greenish cast.

"We're fine!" he whispered harshly. "Now relax!"

Out the window, he could see his friends getting out of the car, horsing around. In the light from the porch he saw Hunt scoop up a handful of snow and try to shove it down the front of Brooke's coat.

154

Brooke was laughing, Cameron was glowering. Some things never changed, not even after you just killed somebody.

Then came the loud footsteps on the wooden porch, the stomping of feet as they tried to rid their boots of snow. And then, the pounding on the door.

"Hey, Jack!" It was Hunt calling. "Yoo-hoo!"

"Get the door," Jack told Jill. She didn't move. *"Get it!"*

She started toward the door. Then stopped, pointing down in horror. Jack turned to see what she was pointing at. He had to take the towel off his head before he spotted it.

There was a half-moon shape of thick blood that had seeped from Martin's head into the white sofa cushion. It was like the big red X they put on maps. The stain said, "Martin Was Murdered *Here*."

Jill was already moving before Jack could think what to do. She yanked down the plaid blanket that was draped over the back of the sofa, crumpling it so that it looked natural. But she made sure it covered the stain.

The pounding on the door grew louder. And when Jack turned back to the door, he saw Hunt's face peering ghoulishly through the living-room window.

Jack waved. Jill crossed to the front door. And then his friends burst into the room, stamping their feet, laughing, a blast of noise and fun and happiness. A blast from the past, from the normal world he and Jill had just left behind. His friends all stopped laughing as they looked at Jack.

"Hey, guys," he said as cheerfully as he could muster.

"Jack!" Dede said as she hurried across the living room toward him. "What happened?"

"What do you mean?"

155

"Your head," Jill said quickly. "The cut on your forehead."

"You're sooo macho," cooed Brooke. "'What do you mean?' he says. If it's me, and I've got a scratch, I'm fainting."

"That's the truth," agreed Cameron.

"Let me guess," Hunt told Jack. "Jill bit you."

Jack laughed. "Actually, that's not that far off. Hi, Cam. Hi, Bradford."

"Hey," Bradford said. He had unzipped his blue down parka, uncovering his big belly. He had his hands in his pockets. He looked concerned.

"It's really not as bad as it looks," Jack said. "You see what happened was"—he chuckled—"I'm embarrassed to tell you this. Jill, can I tell them? I mean, do you mind?"

Jill didn't answer.

"Ooh," said Brooke, sitting down on the sofa right next to the blanket that covered the blood. "I smell trouble." She started nervously picking at the gray strands of wool that fringed the blanket. Jack had to force himself to look away.

"We were having a little argument, as I guess you guys already picked up on," Jack confessed.

"Bingo," said Brooke.

"Join the club," said Cameron.

"I got a little frisky, ha-ha, and—" Jack put on a hangdog expression. "We were jousting with the fire pokers and—"

"And I won," Jill finished with a broad smile. To Jack, that smile looked ghastly. But everyone laughed.

Everyone laughed—except Hunt. He had that sparkle in his eyes that he got when he was gearing up for some major teasing. "Jousting with pokers, eh?" he asked, doing a British accent. He mimed holding a pipe. "A likely story, eh, Watson?"

He poked Bradford in the belly.

"Huh?"

"Oh, come now, Watson," Hunt continued. "You can't be as stupid as all that."

Bradford gave him a quick shove that sent Hunt skittering several steps toward Brooke. He landed next to her on the sofa, which meant he was sitting right on the blanket. Luckily, he got up again. "For instance," he said, continuing with his accent, "I spy with my little eye that there is only one poker over by that fireplace. So! The idea of the two of you jousting with pokers would have to be, shall we say, a total lie?"

He finished with a flourish and a bow. Only Brooke applauded.

"Seriously," Hunt said, poking Jack with a forefinger. "What's the story, huh? huh? huh?"

Jack tried to get away, but Hunt kept after him, and since he was holding the towel to his wound, Jack couldn't maneuver very well. "I-I thought she had the poker. Maybe she had—"

"The shovel," Jill said. She held up the other tool that was stored in the metal bucket next to the fireplace.

"The shovel?" Hunt echoed. "But would that cut Jack's head like this? It's flat."

"Well it did!" Jack snarled.

There was a silence.

"You got anything to eat?" Bradford asked.

"Check the kitchen," Jack said. "But I doubt it. Hey, I've got an idea. Why don't we all go to a movie? Or there's duckpins not too far from here. Jill and I are feeling kind of cooped up."

"Cooped up?" asked Brooke. "You just got here. Boy, I was right. You really aren't getting along, are you? See, Cameron, we're normal."

157

Cameron turned on the TV and stared at it, flipping the channels.

"Wait a minute," Hunt said, leaping back to his feet. "I believe I've hit on another problem with your story."

"Hunt, can that accent, will you?" Jack said. "It's really driving me up the—"

Hunt ignored the request. "You say you cut him with the shovel, right, Jill?"

"Yeah, uh, right."

"I don't buy it, but we'll let it pass. But! Where's the blood? If you cut him, shouldn't there be blood on the floor?"

"We cleaned up the blood," Jack snapped. "What's the matter with you?"

Hunt grinned happily. Dropping the accent, he said, "So where's your shadow?"

"My what?"

"You *know*—your number-one friend."

"He means where's Martin," Brooke explained. She leaned her head back on the sofa, letting her mouth hang open like a corpse. "Hey, Bradford, if you find anything in there that's bad for me, bring it to me, would ya?"

"Hunt," said Dede, ignoring the crowd. "Why do you keep walking away from me every time I come near you?"

Hunt was right, she *was* whining. Well, it was his own fault.

"I told you," Jack told Hunt. "We gave Martin the slip."

"Finally," said Jill with another fake smile.

"Amen," said Brooke.

"I don't know," said Dede. "I kind of hate to think of that poor guy all alone on campus over break."

"Are you kidding?" Brooke said. "Remember how

158

mad Jack was in the gym? The guy's lucky he's not up here, man. If he goes too far, Jack would kill him. Wouldn't you, Jack?"

"Yeah," Jack said, smiling sweatily. "I probably would."

"I predict he snuffs it," Hunt said, leaning against the fireplace and patting the moose. "In fact, I'll take two-to-one odds. Any takers?"

A moment ago, Jack had been petrified that Hunt was onto them. But now Hunt was placing bets on Martin's suicide plans—that was good news indeed.

Bradford came back from the kitchen with a half-empty bag of popcorn. He was chewing as he held the bag out to Brooke. "Stale," he told her. "There's like nothing in your cupboards," he told Jack.

"I know," Jack said. "That's why I think we should go out."

No one looked too excited by the idea.

"Hey, guys?" Brooke said. "Could everyone lighten up here? I mean, we're on vacation. We're away from that awful place—I won't say the word, but it begins with a *B*. No rules, guys, remember? We can do what we want."

"I want to watch TV," Cameron grumbled. He was sitting with his head about a foot from the screen.

"Oh, wow," said Hunt.

Brooke screamed.

That didn't mean anything. Brooke loved to scream.

Jack turned with an almost insane calm. "What's wrong?" he asked.

Hunt was looking at the sofa.

The blanket had fallen off. There was the stain.

Everyone stared at it. Then Hunt turned and looked at Jack.

"We're going to catch hell," Jack said, his eyes locked on Hunt's. "Look, Jill—I messed up my dad's favorite sofa."

CHAPTER 23

"JACK," DEDE SAID, "LET ME SEE THAT CUT. I'm serious. Take off the towel. C'mon."

Dede's interest in the cut was distracting everyone from the sofa, but other than that, it was driving Jack crazy.

"I'm fine!"

"I don't know, Jack. I think we better take you to a hospital," she said.

Hospital. That meant records. Which could mean someday explaining to some cops how he got that cut. You see, officer, as I told my friend, my girlfriend and I were jousting with pokers. Well, a poker and a shovel actually.

"Hospital, bowling, whatever," said Hunt, plopping back down on the bloodstained sofa. "Just as long as we're all together, right, guys?"

Jack was staring at Jill, hoping for help. She shrugged miserably. He was on his own.

"C'mon, Jack," Dede said gently, "let me."

There was no way around it. He let go of the towel. She delicately pulled it away from the wound. She gasped. So did everyone else in the room.

"You're going to need some stitches, buddy," Cameron told him, peering at the cut.

"Major stitches," agreed Brooke.

"They're going to have to chop off your head," joked Hunt.

"Jill?" Jack said.

She was supposed to say something about how minor the cut looked. But instead she said, "It does look pretty bad." Then she looked away. She sat down on the old leather hassock, propping her head up with one hand. It was as if the blood that Jack was losing were coming from Jill's body, because she was looking even paler than before.

As pale as Martin after they—

"All right," Jack said, stepping back from his friends and waving a hand in the air to shoo them away. "I'll go up the hill to the lodge. Mrs. Dobb has a whole first-aid kit."

"I'm coming with you," Bradford said firmly, leaving no room for argument.

They all went. And as they followed the dirt road Hunt started clapping his big yellow gloves together and singing. "Jack and Jill went up the hiiil. . . ."

Still holding the towel to his head, Jack called after him, "Shut up, Hunt, okay? You're really giving me a pain."

"To fetch a pail of waterrrrrr . . . Jack fell down and broke his crown and—" Hunt chased after Jill, caught her, and tickled her. He kept singing. "Jill came tumbling . . . after!" Jill didn't laugh, though, not even when he lifted her in the air. "What's the matter, Jill?" teased Hunt. "Somebody forget to plug you in tonight?"

"She's just upset from her fight," Brooke stage-whispered.

Jill turned away. Talk about acting suspicious. Was she *trying* to give them away?

And the looks she kept giving Jack. Furtive accusing glances. As if they hadn't planned this whole murder together.

It took Mrs. Dobb several minutes to answer the knocker on the lodge front door. Jack peered through the curtained window and saw the little old woman tying the belt on her thick cotton robe as she came down the front steps.

"Hi," Jack said, when she opened the door, "I'm really sorry to bother you, Mrs. Dobb, but I had a little accident and—"

"Oh, my goodness," Mrs. Dobb said. "Come in, come in."

"Mrs. Dobb, these are some of my friends that stopped by to see us. This is—"

But Mrs. Dobb had him by the hand and was leading him quickly back to the office. She reached over the half door to unlock it. "Sit here," she said. He sat.

Everyone had trooped into the room after them, trailing snow and slush off their shoes, cold air seeping out of the crevices of their bulky coats. Mrs. Dobb opened a tall freestanding metal closet and pulled out a large blue-and-white first-aid kit, which she set on her cluttered desk.

"Is he going to live, Doc?" Hunt asked her.

"I doubt it," Mrs. Dobb said. She stuck a Q-Tip into a large brown bottle of antiseptic. The cotton tip came out red as blood. And when she swabbed the cotton stick on Jack's cut, the pain was fantastic.

Jack yelped. "What is that?" he demanded. "Vinegar?"

Instead of answering, Mrs. Dobb swabbed on some more of the gruesome red stuff. "Now, what in heaven's name were you doing to get yourself a cut like this?"

Jack twitched and grimaced.

"That's a good question," Hunt said. Jack didn't like the suspicious look on his face, didn't like it one bit.

"They were playing and his girlfriend accidently hit him in the head with a shovel," Dede explained innocently.

Or was it innocently? Everything everyone said was starting to sound suspicious to Jack.

"They were having a major fight," Brooke corrected. "And his girlfriend Jill here tried to kill him, basically."

Jill whirled on her. But whatever she was going to say, she held it back. Still, her anger was clear, and to Jack, it seemed almost insanely inappropriate.

"See what I mean?" Brooke told Mrs. Dobb with an easy laugh. "They're both on edge."

Mrs. Dobb, cotton swab held aloft, was staring at Jill, sharp eyes narrowed. "So you're the girlfriend?"

All eyes on Jill now. Who looked like she was about to pass out. She didn't respond.

"Well?" Mrs. Dobb said with a mean chuckle. "Are you the girlfriend or not?"

Jill's eyes met Jack's. He felt like his whole life hung in the balance, like she could betray him right then and there.

Then she shook off his gaze and looked back at Mrs. Dobb, wrinkling her nose, rabbit-style. "That's me," she said.

Mrs. Dobb turned back to Jack. In an almost conversational tone, she said, "Seriously, Jack, how'd you cut yourself?"

"We were playing tag outside and I—*ow!*—ran into a rock." Jack glared at Hunt. "And *that's* the truth," he said.

Hunt winked.

"Does he need stitches?" Dede asked. She had her hand on his shoulder, which felt good, Jack had to admit. He looked for Jill. He hoped she wasn't noticing. He certainly didn't need her to get any madder.

Jill was standing at the door, facing out into the woods. Right away, Jack knew what she was thinking, what she was feeling. The feeling was mutual. Because as soon as he saw her back, so tense, he also saw the back of Martin's head caving in.

"I don't think stitches will be necessary," Mrs. Dobb said. "But I'll put on one of these big Band-Aids." She held up a brown bandage for Jack to see. "They call this a butterfly." She leaned her head closer. She smelled like old cedar chips. "Don't worry, Jack. I won't tell Daddy on you. As long as you're very very good to me!"

She laughed uproariously. Jack didn't like the shrewd look in her eye.

"Wow," Bradford said. He was examining Mrs. Dobb's computer. "This looks like a screamer. What is it? A 386?"

"Four eighty-six," she told him proudly. "With an internal modem. I've been spending my whole winter in cyberspace, you might say. You know, playing around with bulletin boards, Internet, that sort of thing. But David Cronenberg, he's one of my renters? He's a computer specialist, and he tells me—hold still, Jack. There! He tells me that in a year tops all the IBM stuff is going to be totally obsolete. Everyone's going to have this power-chip thingamajig so they can run Mac and IBM at the same time. All the DOS stuff will be replaced by Windows."

"Fascinating," Hunt said sarcastically.

Bradford's mouth was hanging open. Now he grinned at Jack. "Hey," he said, jerking a big thumb at Mrs. Dobb. "This lady's conversant. She knows it all. How'd ya learn?"

Mrs. Dobb smiled proudly. "Oh, I've been teaching myself these past few years. I started when Mount Pinkney shut down. That was the handwriting in the snow, you might say. Now Mount Rose." She smiled. "Look at me. I'm seventy-six, and I'm still worrying about having something to fall back on! If only I could have some of Jack's money, right, Jack?" She smiled at him. He frowned. Then she patted him. "You're all set."

He didn't feel all set. He felt like he was going to swoon to the floor. The heat of the lodge, the intense pressure of trying to hide Martin's body—

"Up we go," Bradford said, pulling him up out of the chair.

It was a horrible night. As soon as they got back to the chalet, Brooke tried to get a drink of water and discovered that the water was off.

"I thought you said you cleaned up?" she asked slyly.

"That's right," Jack said.

"With what?" asked Dede, with her usual maddeningly sweet expression.

"We borrowed water," Jill answered for him.

"Borrowed water?" asked Cameron.

"From a neighbor," Jack said testily. "What's the matter with you guys, anyway?"

Hunt's fox eyes were gleaming. "What's the matter with *us*?"

There was a question pounding in Jack's brain. Just how much had Hunt seen when they first arrived, when he looked in the window . . . ?

That night, Jill excused herself early, saying she

was having stomach cramps. Jack tried to come upstairs with her, but Jill said no. Everyone was watching. No way to really talk.

"You're sure you're okay?" he asked, trying to put as much meaning behind the words as he could.

"Yeah."

Soon after, Brooke and Dede went up to bed, sleeping in the same room as Jill, so there was no way Jack could get to her.

He ended up sleeping in the bottom bunk of the smallest bedroom. Big Bradford insisted on the top bunk. It wasn't the greatest feeling having that huge weight lying above him. If these flimsy bunks didn't hold, Jack was a dead man.

Bradford snored like a small engine.

The next morning, Jack woke up drenched in sweat. He could hear Jill arguing with Brooke downstairs. Brooke asked Jill, "What are you guys hiding, anyway?" Jack hurried down the steps.

The first person he saw was Dede. She had a sponge in one hand, a Styrofoam cup filled with snow in the other; she was scouring away the bloodstain on the sofa.

Then he saw Jill. She was standing in between Brooke and the closed basement door, as if ready to guard it with her life. The rest of his friends were lounging around the living room, watching the scene with what looked like dazed surprise. Brooke looked up at Jack.

"Your girlfriend's crazy," she said. "All I wanted to do is check out the basement. Maybe your dad keeps snowshoes or cross-country skis down there. I thought we'd go for a little morning hike, and she starts acting like there's radiation down there or something."

"I just know there aren't any skis down there," Jill said.

"Then why can't I look?"

"Yeah," agreed Hunt, springing to his feet. He tossed down the yellowed newspaper he must have taken off the fireplace stack and sauntered toward Jill. "Why can't we look?"

"Of course you can look," Jack said. "Jill, chill out. Let 'em look—my dad won't care." He squeezed her shoulder. She looked at him with disbelief. He opened the door partway, till it nudged her back, then she got out of the way.

Jack went down first. He was smiling, but inside he was seething. How stupid could Jill get?

By now, Jill had managed to create such intense interest in the basement that even Cameron and Bradford trudged down the steps to see what was up.

"Well, lookie here," Brooke said.

Jack followed her gaze. Leaning up against the far wall was an assorted array of old skis and snowshoes and sleds.

Brooke crossed her arms. "No skis, Jill?"

"I . . . I . . ."

"She just didn't want you coming down here," Jack said, "because, uh, my dad doesn't like people in the basement."

"Oh, I believe *that* one," Hunt said. He was looking at the huge white freezer. It was hard not to look at it. Pale and gleaming, it dominated the whole basement space like some huge ghostly coffin.

"All right!" Cameron said, rubbing his hands together, "maybe there's some breakfast in there."

"But it's frozen," Jill said. "I mean, it's empty. I mean—"

"Jill," Jack said, "re-lax. If they want to look in the freezer, let them look in the freezer." He was talking slowly, as if to a two-year-old.

"I'll tell ya," Bradford rumbled. "Right now I'm feeling hungry enough to eat a whole mess of frozen veal chops."

Hunt moved toward the large white freezer, pushing Jack out of the way. "Excuse me, *Captain?*"

Jack had never liked the way Hunt called him captain. Hunt thought he himself should have been elected to the post, and whenever he called Jack captain it always had a slight edge to it. But this time the word sounded like an open threat.

Jill covered her mouth with her hand.

Jack's mouth had gone dry. He stepped back. "Be my guest."

Hunt studied his face in the basement's gloomy half-light, then stepped forward almost cautiously toward the freezer.

Jack could feel the tension in the room. It was as if everyone already knew what was hidden inside that white metal box. He was standing near the wall. Next to him leaned a large wooden-handled shovel. Hunt had his back to him as he bent over and fumbled with the latch on the freezer's lid. Then suddenly he turned and looked back at Jack, as if he thought Jack was about to brain him one.

Then he turned back to the freezer. He opened the lid with both hands.

The rubber seal made a sucking sound as it opened.

Then Hunt turned back to look at all of his friends.

His mouth was hanging open.

CHAPTER 24

"IT'S EMPTY," HUNT SAID.

Jill's eyes were wide. She stood on tiptoes, peering down into the empty freezer.

"What'd I tell you?" said Jack.

Hunt shrugged. "The way you guys were acting so jumpy, I was sure you had something major stashed down here."

Jack closed the freezer with a bang. "C'mon," he said. "Let's drive into town. I'm starving."

It was true. He had that hunger he usually got after a big game, when everything had gone his way and he could finally relax.

It was over, he told himself. They had done it.

Last night, he had quietly tiptoed downstairs like a kid sneaking down to peek at his Christmas presents. He had driven the body back to Braddington.

On the way, Jack had gotten the distinct feeling that someone was following him. Feeling half-crazy with paranoia, he made several sharp turns, pulled a U-ee, drove around a factory parking lot, and executed several other escape maneuvers. The dark car disappeared from his rearview mirror.

He drove fast, though the idea of getting a ticket was pretty terrifying, with a half-frozen stiff thawing in the trunk.

Just as he had planned, he put Martin's stuff—suitcase and hat—on the footbridge. Then he dropped Martin's body down into the Passonic. He landed on his back, making it seem as if one of these rocks had bashed in his head. Even an autopsy couldn't catch them now.

Three weeks later Jack Washburn III sat on a metal stool at the counter of Greasy Betty's, an empty glass of water in front of him.

"You're sure you don't want to order?" the waitress asked him. She was a short bowlegged woman with a dangling cigarette and a wrinkled face.

"I'll wait."

"Doesn't look like your girlfriend's going to show."

He looked over her shoulder at the clock. Then down at his hand. It was trembling.

Then the door slammed, and Jack swiveled hard on his stool, a smile bursting across his face when he saw Jill inside the door.

His smile faded fast. She had dark circles under her eyes. Her cheeks were sunken. She didn't even meet his gaze.

"Hi, Jack," she said tonelessly.

"Hi." He stood. "C'mon," he said. "Let's take a booth."

They ordered. A double burger, onion rings, fries, and a shake for Jack, nothing for Jill.

"First of all," Jack said, "I just want to say, I am really sorry I didn't call you earlier, but—"

"That's okay," she said. The way she said it made Jack's heart plummet. It sounded like it would be okay if he never called her again.

171

After the torturous weekend at the chalet, Jack had dropped Jill back at her house, then driven straight home to Groton and—

"Jill," he said. "It's like I went zombie. I was holed up in my room. I came out for food and calls of nature."

"I said," Jill repeated, "it's okay."

It was their first day back after winter break, the day that was supposed to mark their new beginning. As soon as Jack had returned to campus, he had called Jill. Seeing their old haunts, he'd suddenly found himself dying to see her, kiss her, hold her. But now— The pauses and silences stretched longer and longer. He checked his watch. They didn't have much time left. This afternoon there was a special assembly to commemorate Martin's death. Attendance was required.

"Jill," he said. "I know this has been rough, but we're out of the woods, Rabbit. You know that, don't you? We're free."

He reached for her hand, but she pulled it free. Just then, the waitress brought the food, slapping it down on the speckled Formica tabletop. Jack didn't make a move to eat.

Abruptly, Jill pitched to her feet, as if she were going to bolt out of the diner. Then she sat back down, looked away from him, and said, "You . . . You just don't get it, do you?"

"Get it? Get what?"

"What we did!"

She had raised her voice. Both teenagers turned to see if anyone was listening. The waitress was talking to another customer, dribbling cigarette ash over his cherry pie. Jill looked straight at him now.

"I mean," Jill said in a whisper, "don't you feel *anything*, Jack? Don't you feel even a little sorry, for what you did?"

172

Jack smiled. He didn't mean to smile, it was a bad habit he had sometimes, when he was really tense. "What *I* did? Jill, it was both of us, okay? Just for starters. Okay? Jill?"

She started out of the booth again, but he grabbed her arm, pulling her back down.

"You're so crazy—I tried to stop you!" she said.

"No, you didn't. You didn't! You *pretended* to try and stop me so you could feel less guilty later. Who knows? Maybe you wanted to pin the whole thing on me. But you wanted him dead just as much as I did. Don't kid yourself."

"You're a psychopath."

"Takes one to know one."

They sat silently glowering at each other. Jack picked up the burger, some grease running down his wrist. He tossed it back on the plate. And then all at once, he laughed. The irony was just too great.

Her eyebrows went up, but this was one joke he wasn't going to share.

They had killed Martin to save their future.

And now—it looked pretty clear—there was nothing left to save.

"Every suicide is a cry for help," intoned Reverend Morrissey. "But none of us heard Martin Rucker's cry. We all must live with that guilt. Every last one of us. For we are all God's children. And just as a father loves each one of his children, so does our Heavenly Father love us all. To take one's own life—"

The reverend, who was looking pale and haggard, lost her voice for a moment. "To take one's own life is the—perhaps the worst crime we can commit. Worse than murder."

Jack glanced to his right. He was relieved to see

173

ERIC WEINER

Wallace Wasserman back in his normal seat. Who did he expect to be sitting there? he thought wildly. Martin's ghost?

The reverend was crying. Jack couldn't look. He lowered his head. Maybe they'd think he was praying.

After an awkward pause, during which the reverend's little halting cries were broadcast over the microphone through the entire auditorium, Dean Schmidt replaced the reverend at the podium. "I just want to say that each and every one of us on the faculty, and I'm sure each and every one of you, is deeply shocked and saddened by Martin Rucker's death. Um. Mr. Pardee would like me to announce that the guidance department is offering counseling sessions for any students who want or need to talk about this horrible loss. The guidance department will be open all day this week and next week as well, from eight A.M. until check-in. So please, people, if you're feeling bad, don't try to face this alone."

And now the dean was getting choked up, too. But that wasn't what shocked Jack. Suddenly Jack felt the hot tears welling up in his own eyes. Three weeks of feeling nothing, and now—

A horribly sad thought had occurred to him.

Martin would have been so amazed and delighted that people were getting teary about his being gone. He never would have believed it.

"And now," said the dean. He ran his hands over his crew cut a few times, trying to regain his composure. "And now, Martin's father . . . would like to . . . uh . . . say a few words."

Oh, no, thought Jack. Not the father. Please, not the father.

Mr. Rucker was a short man, like his son, but age had given him stature, as perhaps it might have done for Martin himself. Mr. Rucker had silver hair and

174

spectacles and steel-blue eyes. He shook the dean's hand vigorously, then stepped to the mike.

"I won't be long," he began softly. "The dean has counseled me that in tragedies such as this, there is sometimes a copycat effect, whereby other young people are provoked into . . . taking their own lives as well. If Martin's death has served any purpose at all—" He started to cry.

He's faking! thought Jack. He wanted to jump up and yell it. Faker!

Mr. Rucker checked his notes. "Any purpose at all, I would like to think that he would serve as an inspiration to all of you. My young friends . . . we must learn to open up to one another. We cannot face our sorrows by ourselves."

An astonishing thing was happening to Jack. The tears had not subsided, they had gotten worse. It was as if the tears were gathering together to form one huge wave. And then . . .

Jack sprang a leak. It was as if the ugly scar on his forehead had opened up and was gushing tears instead of blood, dripping them down both cheeks. His classmates were putting hands on his shoulders, trying to see if he was okay. This caused enough commotion to turn nearby heads, and cause those seated in the balcony to peer down and see what all the fuss was about.

Jack got to his feet. Mumbling, "Excuse me, excuse me," he stumbled over the feet of his fellow students and made his way down the aisle. He hurried up the long stone rampway, past hundreds of curious faces, heading out the door.

Through his tears, he could see the girls growing restless. They were making way for a student. Jill was coming after him.

Onstage, Mr. Rucker was continuing with his

175

speech, ignoring the interruption with a practiced ease. Mr. Simmons caught up with Jack just before he pushed out through the double exit doors.

"Jack," Mr. Simmons said harshly. And then he hugged Jack hard.

Over Mr. Simmons's shoulder, Jack could see Jill, hurrying toward them.

Mr. Simmons pushed Jack back to arm's length. "Remember what I told you, boy. It wasn't your fault. You understand me?"

Jack nodded.

"It wasn't your fault!"

Jack turned and pushed out the door, head down. Once outside, he started to jog. It was a freezing January afternoon. The air cut his lungs with every breath. But he didn't stop running until he had reached the steps to the library. He sat down. He held his head in his hands.

A few minutes later Jill's black winter boots appeared in his line of vision. He looked up.

"Brilliant," she said.

"I couldn't help it," he said. It came out like a moan.

"No," she said. "I'm serious. That was brilliant. If anyone had any doubts about us, that little performance will end them once and for all. You looked so utterly grief-stricken. You should go out for Dramat, Jack."

"B-but, I wasn't faking."

Jill sat down wearily next to him. "Right. I accuse you of being cold, so you burst into tears. Very subtle."

Jack wiped his face. "That's not true. I'm really *sad* about this. I mean, why can't you believe that?"

"Why do you think?"

He lowered his head. She had a point.

"After everything Rucker told us about his dad," he

176

said, sniffing loudly, "it made me crazy hearing the guy BS us like that. Like he cared about Martin. He used to beat the kid."

"Jack, we didn't treat him too kindly either."

Jack looked at her, his mouth hanging open, his face gripped with pain. There was no love in the face that stared back.

Maybe he'd get it back, somehow—her love.

Or maybe that was just one of the things he'd have to give up to pay for Martin's death.

That evening, Jack was lying on his water bed, the lights off, staring up at the parachute canopy as it billowed in the darkness. There was a soft familiar knock at the door.

He lifted his head as the door opened.

And Martin Rucker walked into the room.

CHAPTER 25

"OH, GOD!" JACK GASPED, SHRINKING BACK.

"I'm so sorry to disturb you," said a lilting, familiar voice. "It's just—"

It felt like someone was dribbling a big basketball on top of Jack's chest. His heart was pounding mercilessly. Then he saw that it wasn't Martin at all. It was a woman, about Martin's height. She had short mousy-brown hair.

"Let me just . . ." Jack got up, stumbling over to the desk to get the light.

"I'm so sorry to wake you," said the woman politely.

"You didn't wake me," Jack said.

"I'm Elaine Giddings, Martin's mother."

"I'm Jack, Jack Washburn."

Past the woman and through the open doorway, Jack could see into Martin's room. It had been totally cleaned out. The dark empty space was ominous and threatening, like a giant grave.

"I know who you are," Mrs. Giddings said. "Mr. Simmons tells me that you were Martin's closest friend in the dorm." She looked down. "He probably told you all sorts of horrible things about me."

"No," Jack lied. "Not at all. Only nice things. Wonderful things."

He had laid it on too thick. "That's a lie," she said coldly. "But I thank you for it. I suppose I have no right to grieve, considering how little involvement I've had in my son's life until now."

"I'm sure you did the best you could."

"No, I don't think I did, actually. Anyway." She gave an odd smile. "I just wanted to say thank you. I know my son was a difficult and troubled boy. Mr. Simmons says you're one of the most popular students in the dorm, but that you went out of your way to be nice to Martin. God bless you for that. God bless you for doing what I should have done."

There was no emotion in the woman's voice, Jack noticed. He shivered.

And then the woman stepped forward, and Jack had to work hard to keep from ducking backward again. His first thought was that she was going to strike him.

Instead she planted a soft kiss on his cheek. Then stood awkwardly for a moment more. Then turned and left.

Jack waited until he heard the stairwell door open and shut, then he went down to the bathroom to wash off his face.

But the feel of the woman's dry chapped lips stayed with him through the night.

Jack was still up four hours later. It was way past lights-out. He didn't bother to put a towel under his door. He was sitting in the wing chair, the chair Martin had sat in so often. Then he heard footsteps and a soft, scraping sound as something was shoved under his door.

Jack stood. He moved toward the door and looked down. From the floor, a large bald man smiled up at him. He stared at the face uncomprehendingly.

Someone had slipped a record cover into his room. *Uncle Phil Sings Your Favorite Nursery Rhymes.*

Jack bent down and picked up the cover.

The song title "Jack and Jill" had been circled in red.

Jack flung open his door. But whoever had left him the little present was already gone.

CHAPTER 26

THAT FIRST WEEK BACK AT SCHOOL WENT BY in a nightmarish blur. Jack was having both cold sweats and sudden hot flashes. It was as if his own body had become some kind of crazy weather storm. Every morning he woke up with the desperate hope that it was all a dream. Once he even woke up yelling, "Please!"

Please let it be that . . . Martin wasn't dead.

Please let it be that Jack hadn't murdered a fellow student in cold blood.

Please.

What were his reasons for killing Martin? They no longer seemed obvious. In fact, Jack could not believe that it was he—Jack—who had done such a thing at all. When he replayed the scene in his mind—or, as it happened more often, when it replayed itself—it was as if he were watching an actor in the role of Jack. Not him. Not him at all. And that actor was vicious and crazy.

As crazy as Martin.

But the days went by. And life went on at Braddington as if Martin had never existed. A new kid, a transfer student from Choate, moved into 3-H. He was a jolly black-haired third former named Stuart Miles. Jack rarely spoke to him.

Time heals all, Reverend Morrissey had said in her sermon. Well, time didn't seem to be doing too good a job on Jack's guilt. What did he expect? he asked himself. To kill someone and feel nothing at all? No. He would have to live with what he had done for the rest of his life. But at least . . .

He would live with the crime in private. Surely, that was the silver lining in all of this horror. At least he and Jill had gotten away with the crime! Slowly, slowly, Jack's mood began to lift.

One Monday night, while he was working at his terminal, typing a paper for McNulty on the many conspiracy theories about the Kennedy assassination, he even started to sing. Then he realized what he was singing.

"Jack and Jill."

Jack shook his head. He grinned.

The computer beeped twice.

He looked back at the console.

An E-mail note had popped up at the top of the screen:

SO, JACK. I KNOW YOU DIDN'T LIKE THE GUY. BUT HEY—DID YOU HAVE TO *KILL* HIM?

Jack nearly fell over in his chair.

He stumbled to his feet, backing away from the computer.

Then he whirled around, suddenly convinced there was someone in the room watching him.

There was.

"Sorry," his neighbor Stuart told him. "Didn't mean to startle you. I just wanted to ask you a ques-

182

tion. How strict are they around here about hot plates in the room? I mean I know it's in the rule book and all, but, you know, is that like one of those things that Simmons has a hissy over or—"

Jack pushed by him. Then he reached back and pulled his door shut, checking the knob to make sure it had locked. "Ask your proctor," he said as he headed off down the hall.

"Hey," Stuart called after him. "It doesn't hurt to be friendly to your hallmates, you know."

"Go suck an egg," Jack called back.

He was slapping the wall as he walked. He burst into Hunt's room, hitting the half-open door with his shoulder so that the door banged back against the wall. The doorknob chipped off a small piece of plaster.

Hunt was at his computer. Cameron and Bradford were there as well, all studying for their bio test. They looked up, startled. Jack shoved Hunt hard, so that his chair tipped. Hunt had to drop his notebook and grab the desk with both hands to right himself. "You think you're funny, huh, Lowry?" Jack said. "Huh? You think you're funny?"

He shoved him again. Hunt slapped his hand away. "I think I'm hysterical, actually," Hunt said. "But you've got the wrong room. Bellevue is further down the hall."

"Shut up!"

Bradford had stood up now. He had his big hand on Jack's shoulder. But Jack spun free. He got right in Hunt's face. "You telling me you didn't just net me?"

"*Net* you?" Hunt echoed, making it sound like the most ludicrous word in the English language. "Net you? Does anyone have any idea what this guy is talking about?"

"Stop playing dumb!" Jack yelled at him. "You didn't just send me that E-mail?"

"Noooo," Hunt said with a loopy smile.

"How about that record cover two weeks ago? You telling me that wasn't from you?"

"Record cover . . ." Hunt tapped his chin thoughtfully. "It sounds like a wonderful gift, Captain, but I can't take the credit."

"And knock off that captain crap! Wrestling season is over, in case you hadn't noticed."

"Jack," Cameron said. "What's the matter with you? Calm down."

Jack paced around the room. "I can't calm down!"

"We can see that," Hunt said, laughing.

Jack started toward him, but Bradford blocked the way, and one big hand from Bradford on Jack's chest was enough to hold him back.

Hunt threw back his head and cackled. "Guys. Get the butterfly nets! Jack's doing a Martin."

Jack charged so abruptly that Bradford didn't have time to react. He tackled Hunt and knocked him down onto the floor. He was about to punch his lights out, but Cameron caught his fist and held it. Hunt was still laughing.

Jack was up half the night.

He couldn't sleep Tuesday night either.

Just like Martin, he thought as he lay trembling in his bed. It was a punishment. He'd get to feel just how Martin felt. Next he'd start hoarding his food and staying in his room all day. And then—

Jack had the lights out. The only light in the room came from his terminal. Which had just beeped twice.

He got out of bed and walked slowly over to the computer. He didn't want to look.

IF YOU WANT ME TO KEEP QUIET ABOUT WHAT I KNOW, LEAVE $50,000 AT YOUR FATHER'S CHALET THIS SUNDAY. CASH, OF COURSE. THANKS EVER SO. NO FOOLING, JACK. IT'S THE BUCKS, OR I GO STRAIGHT TO THE COPS. TA-TA FOR NOW.

Jack flicked off the terminal and rushed out of the room.

CHAPTER 27

BUT HUNT'S ROOM WAS DARK. AND WHEN Jack pressed an ear against the door, he couldn't hear anything inside.

He looked back down the long windowless hall, which was lined with closed dark doors on either side. Whitman had always struck him as being as bleak as a prison. Especially at night, when the overhead lights glowed dully off the hardwood floor. But right now the dorm felt dead. Right then and there, Jack made a decision.

Leaving the dorm after hours without permission, going off campus—it was probably grounds for expulsion. Hey, at Braddington, they could throw you out just for looking at a teacher the wrong way. Jack didn't care. He had to see Jill. In person. Now.

He threw on his winter coat, stuffed his black leather gloves in the pockets, and headed downstairs.

If they could have locked you into your dorm at night, they probably would have. But that would have been a big-time fire hazard. So when Jack pushed on the double front doors, they opened easily.

That was one of the things that had always struck

Jack as so eerie about the academy. There were all these rules, but they were so easy to break. Half the time you could get away with it, too.

He was chuckling crazily as he carefully pulled the double doors shut behind him. Braddington was such a psycho place. They'd probably be just as upset about him going off campus right now as they would be if they knew about the murder.

It wasn't the first time Jack had been off campus at night. His second year at Braddington, he and Cameron had snuck out, just for the thrill of it. They had climbed over the big wrought-iron fence and ran through the shadowy streets of town. They'd ended up at Joe's Diner and had the best hamburgers Jack had ever tasted. That night, the sense of freedom had been delicious. Tonight, he felt like a hunted man.

Twice, he was convinced that he was literally being tracked. He was sure that a car was cruising after him with its lights off. Jack darted across a few snow-covered lawns, slipped between houses. When he came out on the next street, the car was gone.

The homes of Braddington were mainly one- and two-story shingle-style boxes, clustered together on tree-lined streets like the houses in a Monopoly game. It was strange how familiar the streets all seemed to him, as if he walked over to Jill's house all the time. The truth was, Jill had never let him visit. She said she was too embarrassed for him to see where she lived.

He had found her address, though, on a piece of mail that he found in one of her notebooks: 29 Ivy Lane. It was somewhere behind the local firehouse. She had once told him that. Only trouble was, he'd never actually been to Ivy Lane.

Sneaking off campus was such a big crime at Braddington, Jack had sort of figured that once he got out, he'd be able to find Jill's house easily. As he wandered down street after street in the cold, that was starting to seem like a foolish assumption. He stopped on a corner, trying to review his options. He could hike back to the town square and call Jill from a pay phone. He could ask someone. He could . . .

He was staring at the street sign a half block away. He couldn't make out the name, but he could see that the name was short. He headed toward it.

Ivy.

Jill's house was third on the left. Ugly, squat, brown—in the dark it almost looked haunted. Jack knew that Jill was poor, but still, the sight of the little house shocked him.

Even though there were two stories, the house didn't look big enough for Jill to live here alone, let alone for the Marshacks to raise three kids.

Jack walked across the frozen lawn, his shoes cracking through the ice patches. In back, a peeling picket fence enclosed a tiny square yard and a small rusted swing set. Taking off his gloves, Jack dug down through the snow and found a pebble or two. He knew Jill lived on the second floor. The lace curtains on the side window told him the rest.

He rapped three shots off the glass before a light snapped on. Then a ghostly face swam into view. He waved. The face disappeared. The light went off.

Frozen, Jack sat down on a swing, gently rocking back and forth. A minute later Jill slipped quietly out the back door. She was wearing her green overcoat unbuckled over her nightgown. Her bare legs were sticking out of her black vinyl boots.

Jack was so glad to see her he almost cried. He took several quick steps toward her. His arms flew up in the air.

Jill ran into his open arms. For the first time in

weeks she hugged him long and hard. "Oh, I'm so glad you came," she murmured. "How did you know?"

"Know what, Rabbit?"

"That I was missing you."

He noticed she didn't use his old nickname.

Killer.

Jack moved his head, trying to find enough moonlight to see her face clearly. "You're crying," he said. "Oh, sweetie . . ."

He hugged her again, harder.

"I thought you never wanted to see me again," Jill said, crying harder.

"Really? Isn't that funny. That's just what I thought."

Jill pulled her head back again and looked up at him as if to see if he was joking. "I never—" she began. "I mean, I was mad, but—no, no." Another hug. "How could you think that?"

Jill had tears on her cheeks. He wiped them away with his thumb.

"Hey," she said.

"What?"

"You're not supposed to see my ugly old house."

"Too late. And it's not so ugly."

"Yes, it is. It's like a big chocolate wart."

Jack laughed. "Is not."

"Oh, guess what?"

"What?"

"My parents have decided they're really mad at me for not introducing you." She poked his chest. "You're coming over for lunch this Sunday."

The mention of Sunday brought it all back to him, why he was here. That was the day the money was due. "Oh, God," Jack said. Right then, Jill looked so lovely, and the moment was so perfect—or would

189

have been—that he wished he were dead. He hung his head. He had ruined their lives.

Jill was hugging him all over again, kissing his cheek, his ear, reaching under his hood to rake her fingers through his hair. "Hey, Jack," she cooed gently. She shook him slightly. "No, no—no more," she said. "You can't feel guilty about this anymore. We did it, Jack. What's done is done."

"You don't believe that," he said. "You're just saying it to make me feel better."

"No, it's true. I've thought it all through, Jack. You were right. I did want you to . . . do it. And you know what else? As wrong as it was, I still can't see another way we could have gotten out of it. I really can't."

He shook his head sadly, but she grabbed him. She started kissing him hard, fiercely, as if she were trying to kiss the guilt and sadness right out of his body. He pushed her gently away.

"Jill . . . it's not over."

She shivered, studying his face. "What do you mean?"

"It's not done."

"What are you talking about?"

"Someone's blackmailing us."

She didn't say a word. Just waited.

Waited until he had told her everything he knew. Which wasn't much. She rested her head against the cold iron bar of the swing set. "Oh, Jack," she said quietly. She peered at him in the moonlight. "Who could it be?" she asked.

"It's Hunt."

"How do you know?"

"It's Hunt, Jill! Okay? It's Hunt. You saw how he acted that night up at the chalet. He was onto us then. Besides, Hunt has always been a jerk. But Jesus, this is—" He made a fist. "I'm telling you, Jill, I could—"

"Kill him?" Jill asked coldly.

He gave her a sharp look. Then laughed bitterly.

"I'm sorry!" she blurted out, grabbing his hands. "I didn't mean that. Jack?"

He looked at her sadly. "If you turned on me now, Jill, you know what I'd do? I think I would kill myself. I really do. Now wouldn't that be a laugh? If I turned out to be the copycat suicide the faculty was all so worried about?"

"I'm sorry," she said. "It's just a little upsetting."

"Tell me about it."

"So what are we going to do?"

"I don't know. You got any ideas?"

Right away, Jill looked like she was thinking hard. He felt another gush of love for her. That was Jill for you. She never gave up.

"There's something strange here," she finally said.

"Strange?"

"Yeah. I mean, why would Hunt do something like this to you? Isn't he one of your best friends?"

"Yeah. He's also broke, because his parents never give him any money. And on top of that, he's a sadist. When he's wrestling, and he's got his man beat? He never pins him right away. He plays with him until the end of the match, like a cat with a mouse, till the guy's whole face is red with mat burn. You've seen the way he treats Dede, stringing her along."

"I still don't think it's Hunt. Or maybe it is Hunt, I don't know, but it could be any one of your friends, is all I'm saying."

"What are you talking about?"

"Brooke, Cameron, any one of them. They were all at the chalet, right? They all saw how nervous we were, and how I didn't want them down in the basement. What if one of them woke up? Any one of them could have seen you lugging—"

191

She stopped, apparently unable to say *what* he'd been lugging out to the trunk in the middle of that icy awful night. Jack with his hands under Martin's armpits, looking down at the back of Martin's head, all caved in.

"I guess you're right," Jack said. "Any one of them could have seen. But only one of them did. Hunt."

Jack sat down on the swing again, but got back up almost immediately.

"What about Brooke?" Jill asked.

Jack was pacing through the snow. He stopped for a second and stared at her.

"Jack?" she said. "Did you hear me? I said, what about Brooke?"

"What about her?"

"I don't know," Jill said, shivering. "It's just—well, I've always kind of picked up these weird vibes between the two of you. A lot of tension, you know."

"Uh-huh."

Jack was clenching and unclenching his hands. He sighed.

"What?" Jill asked.

He reached out and swung the empty swing with his hand. It made a creepy squeak. It was insane, really. He was feeling as nervous about what he had to tell her as if he were confessing to Martin's murder.

"Once," he began, "when Cameron and Brooke were broken up—sort of . . ."

He let the thought trail off. He didn't want to go on. And from the way Jill was staring at him, he thought he might not have to.

"I don't believe it!" Jill cried. "I was right?"

"It was only once," Jack rushed on. "Here, look, I'll tell you this—everything—and then we'll be done with it, okay? No more questions. We were at this party at the student union, and Cameron was in the infirmary with this horrible flu and—I don't know, one thing led to another."

"What exactly?"

"*Jill* . . . what difference does it make?"

"I want to know what happened."

"No, you don't."

"I want to know!"

"We made out. That's all. For like an hour. Or two. And, I don't know, I guess, afterward, she ended up feeling kind of used, which is sort of ridiculous, right? Because she put the moves on *me*, I swear."

Jill clapped a hand over her mouth as if she were about to scream.

"It's not that big a deal," Jack said. "I swear. I mean, if you think that because of that one incident that Brooke—that she'd want to get this kind of revenge on me—"

"Cameron got sick in September. And you and I—"

"It was right after we met, Jill, we weren't going out yet."

"I thought we were."

Silence.

"Anyway, what does it matter?" Jill asked grimly. "The point is, it's Brooke. She's obviously in love with you. I've known it all along, I just never admitted it to myself."

"No way."

"Believe me. I know."

"Jill, she's just—"

"I thought we had no secrets!" Her voice was strained.

"We don't. Anymore."

"What else haven't you told me?"

"Nothing. Nothing!" Jack insisted.

Jill grabbed his coat with her bare hands. She looked so pained it scared him. "What?" Jack asked.

193

"I just remembered . . . it was Brooke who helped us . . . when we snuck into your room."

"Yeah, right, so?"

"Oh, boy. Ohhh, boy. Brooke must have really loved doing that, considering how she feels about you. God! How could you be so insensitive?"

"It's Hunt," Jack told her. He repeated the name like a drumbeat. "Hunt, Hunt, Hunt."

"What about Cameron?"

"Cameron's my best friend."

"That's what you always say. You guys never even talk."

"So? Guys don't talk. That's a girl thing."

"Don't you think he's kind of angry at you, about Brooke and all?"

"Cameron doesn't know."

"What if he does?"

Jack's head was spinning. The horror was spreading fast inside him like some kind of miracle-grow cancer. Who could he trust? Who?

"What about Dede?" Jill asked.

"Oh, puhlease."

"What?"

"Dede is about the sweetest kid I ever met."

"Thanks a lot."

"Besides you."

"Uh-huh."

"Jill, we don't have time for jealousy, okay? Our whole lives are at stake here, in case you didn't notice."

"I'll say it again. What about Dede?" She was raising her voice again, and Jack was beginning to pray that she hadn't been exaggerating when she said her parents were hard of hearing. He glanced at the house. Still dark.

"C'mon, Jill, you better get inside. You'll catch pneumonia or—"

194

"Get your hands off me. I said, What about Dede? What about Dede!" She was pounding his chest with her fists. He caught her hands and held them. They were like frozen blocks of ice.

"Once," he said miserably.

She gaped at him.

"One kiss, once, last year, way before us."

"I am so humiliated."

"Humiliated? Why?"

"Hanging out with your friends. The dumb townie. The only one who didn't know what was going on."

"*Jill.* You're making way too much of this. Nothing was going on."

Her eyes narrowed. It made his heart flutter. "Last year?" she said. "This was last year?"

"Yeah, uh, you know, when she and Bradford came out to Groton to visit for a weekend."

"Bradford's in love with Dede," Jill said dully. "You always say you love Bradford."

"Yeah. That's what we were talking about, about how Dede should handle the situation, you know, without hurting his feelings and then . . . it just sort of happened."

"I hate your guts."

Jack actually started laughing. She hated him for kissing Dede. He had committed murder. *Murder!*

"Did you hear me, Jack? I said I hate your guts."

"That's nice. But we can take Dede off the list. She has no reason to do this."

"She's probably in love with you, too. And she probably hates the fact that you're going out with me, some poor redneck."

"Jill—"

"And if she can't have you . . ."

"That's absurd."

"And then there's Bradford."

195

"Right. And what about Dean Schmidt? Or Reverend Morrissey? Don't forget them."

"Bradford's a computer hacker."

"No!" Jack cried, shaking a finger in Jill's face. "Okay? If there's one thing I know, I know it's not Bradford." He clutched his head, turning slowly around in circles in the snow. He felt like howling up at the moon.

"Oh, Jill, oh, Jill. I was being so good . . . so good . . . until I met you!"

It was as if he had forgotten he was speaking out loud, forgotten he wasn't alone. Jill stared at him silently, too stung to speak. Then she turned and started back toward the house. He caught her hand. "Wait!"

"Let—go of—me."

"Jill! Listen to me. That was a very stupid thing to say, and I'm sor—Jill! Listen! We can't start fighting. I don't care how mad you are. We've got to stick together on this. We've got to."

She yanked her hand free, but she didn't leave. They stood silently in the darkness, eyeing each other warily.

"Okay," said Jack. "Here's the thing. *Who* is blackmailing us doesn't even matter. Because the thing is, we've got to pay them the money."

"Fifty thousand dollars," muttered Jill, shaking her head.

"How much do you have?" Jack asked.

Jill's jaw dropped. Another stupid thing to ask, Jack knew. But he was desperate.

"Is that some kind of joke?"

"No, I'm afraid it's not."

"I'd have trouble scraping together a hundred dollars. There. Satisfied? Is that what you wanted to hear?"

"No. 'Cause I don't have fifty thousand dollars either."

"Who are you kidding?"

"No one."

"Jack, this is me. I've been to your house, remember? I thought I was in a palace."

"I'm rich on paper, you idiot, not in my wallet!"

Just like that—like he had flicked a light switch—Jill started to cry. So much for not fighting, thought Jack.

"Okay, okay," he said, trying to stay calm. "Okay, okay, okay, okay. I'll just have to sell some stuff. That's all. I'll sell it all. Let's see. The Porsche is old and used. It's a hand-me-down from my dad, but I ought to be able to get, I don't know? Seven thou? This watch cost ten grand. Maybe I could get a tenth of that, that's—"

"Ten thousand dollars? For a watch?"

"It's a Rolex. Keeps perfect time."

Jill was shaking badly. There was no way they could go on talking. He put an arm on her shoulder, but she shook it free. She turned and started toward the door. Jack followed. When she opened the door, she turned back to him. They stood together for a moment in heavy silence. Then Jill went in.

She didn't look back.

CHAPTER 28

"JACK, GLAD YOU COULD JOIN US."

"My pleasure."

"Son, this is Rich Abbisanti."

"Mr. Abbisanti," said Jack, holding his hand out and trying to meet the man's level gaze.

"Jack," said Abbisanti with a tiny smile. He didn't shake hands.

"Have a seat, Jack," said Jack's father.

Jack sat.

It was Wednesday. They were sitting in the black leather banquette in the back of Chez Henri. Jack had called in the reservation, so the waiter had naturally placed them at Jack's usual table. It was the same banquette where Martin had always liked to sit.

It had been a harrowing morning. Word had come to Jack in the middle of Latin class that he was to report to the dean's office as soon as class was over. He had walked up the long flight of marble steps to the administration building like a condemned man marching to the gallows.

When the dean's secretary informed him that Mr. Washburn had flown into Boston and was driving up for a surprise visit, Jack had whooped.

"I guess you miss your dad," the secretary observed, surprised. Most kids at Braddington hated their parents. She told him that he was to make a twelve-thirty reservation at Chez Henri for lunch. For three.

Three? "Are you sure he said for three?" Jack asked the secretary. "Who's the third?"

"I'm sure I don't know," said Mrs. Byers. She was a tall gaunt woman with a bouffant hairdo of silver hair. She was about as warm as most of the staff at Braddington. Another preppy-hating townie.

Three for lunch. The number three had been haunting Jack for hours.

Mr. Washburn was fingering the black leather menu. Then he tossed it back down on the table unopened. He was looking tense, drawn, angry. His jaw was set in stone. Jack knew that look. He'd seen it before—the last two times he'd gotten kicked out of school. Jack was sweating bullets.

The waiter approached the table, giving Jack a familiar smile.

"You know what you want?" his father asked the other man.

Mr. Abbisanti grinned. "You order for me. I don't really know this kind of food."

Rich Abbisanti . . . Jack had never heard his father mention him before. He looked to be in his early forties. Not only that, he looked local. There was a New Hampshire twang to his voice. And the way he held himself—it was like someone who was awfully confident of his ability to beat up any man in the room. Jack could see why. The guy had a barrel chest. He was packed into his suit. A tough character, no doubt about it. Jack's nervousness only grew.

"You know what?" his father told the waiter. "Why don't you bring us—you know—whatever you think best." He handed the waiter the three black leather

199

menus. "Very good, sir," said the waiter. And he was gone.

Jack wanted to call him back and invite the waiter to join them. He could sit in between Jack and the two other men.

The two men were staring at him.

He squirmed.

"I'm glad you could join us on such short notice, Jack," his father said. He didn't sound glad.

"No problem."

"Well, I'm afraid there *is* a problem, Jack. You see—"

He looked up. The waiter had returned and was filling their water glasses. Mr. Washburn waited in steely silence until the waiter was done. The waiter obviously picked up on the way the two men were staring at him. He left in a hurry.

"Do you want to tell my son what you do?" Mr. Washburn asked Abbisanti.

"You do it."

"Rich is a private investigator, Jack."

The words went into Jack's ears and sank like stone right to the bottom of his feet. "I-I don't understand," he said.

"You know what a private investigator is, don't you, Jack?" asked Abbisanti, giving him a mock-quizzical look.

"Yeah, sure, but—"

"One afternoon about a month ago," began Mr. Washburn, "I got a call from your friend, Jack. Martin. I was already worried about you, after the things he said that weekend. But now he tells me *he's* very worried about you, Jack. Says you're sneaking off campus every night. I didn't believe it, of course. I didn't believe my own son would do anything so *stupid*. So I made a phone call and that night—"

He nodded at the detective. Jack turned.

Abbisanti's eyes were boring into Jack's. Jack looked away. He felt like he was going to throw up.

"Mr. Abbisanti followed you up to Blueberry Hill, Jack."

"May I be excused for a moment?"

Mr. Washburn put a hand on his shoulder, pressing him back down into his seat. "Not yet, son."

"Dad, I really think I'm going to be sick. I was up really late last night and—"

"Son, I don't care if you puke your guts out. We're going to talk about this, and we're going to talk about it now. I took time off from a very busy schedule to come up here, and believe me, it wasn't easy to get away. If you want to know if I'm happy about being here, I'll be frank with you. I'm *very upset* about it, okay? So if you don't mind, I'd like to get this over with now. Understood?"

Jack blinked.

"Good," said Mr. Washburn. "Now, Mr. Abbisanti has been filling me in on your 'activities,' shall we say. And it's not pretty, now is it?"

"I don't know what you're talking about, I—"

"Jack, I don't think you're getting the picture. Mr. Abbisanti also followed you *last* night. We know everything that you've been doing, Jack. Everything."

Jack had to wipe away a tear that was leaking out of the corner of his eye. "Dad," he said. "I can explain. I swear I never thought any of this would happen. But it's just like, one thing led to—"

"Sneaking off campus?" Mr. Washburn said, lowering his head to drive the words home. "To be with some townie *slut?*"

Jack sat back, stunned and confused. Was that what was bothering his father? What about the—

"Jack," Mr. Washburn said, "you don't have any conception of the future that lies in store for you, do you? Politics, business, law—whatever field you want . . . Your grandfather and I have worked hard to give you a first-class ticket to the best of society. The riches and the spoils. And what do you do? You throw that ticket in the gutter." Mr. Washburn fumbled with his hands as if he were ripping up an imaginary ticket. "Just throw it away. Like so much garbage!

"Well, some of that we can chalk up to your still being young, I suppose. We've all sowed some wild oats, Jack. Myself included. But there comes a time when I've got to say, this is not wild oats anymore, this is just plain *dumb*. What do you think it would do to any future political aspirations you might have if you were thrown out of Braddington a *third* time? Have you ever thought about that? I wouldn't be able to get you back in. Not this time. That's just for starters."

Jack felt like laughing out loud. They had no idea what he'd done! Dad was just upset because—

"Jack," said the detective.

Stopping midtirade, Mr. Washburn looked over at Mr. Abbisanti. "May I?" the detective asked.

Mr. Washburn nodded. Father and son both looked at the detective, waiting.

The detective smiled at Jack, as if they were going to have a friendly conversation. "What's that on your forehead, Jack?"

Jack had taken to brushing his hair forward, trying to cover the ugly white triangular mark. He nervously pulled his forelock. "This? Nothing. Playing. Stupid." He couldn't get out more than single words.

Abbisanti waited. Finally he went on. "That night you went up to Blueberry Hill. Remember?"

"Yeah, you know, um, vaguely."

"Uh-huh. Well, you went on a little trip in the middle of the night, do you remember that?"

Jack's heart seized midbeat.

"You want to tell your father where you went?" the detective said. It was more of an order than a question.

"I don't know what you're talking about."

"I think you do."

"Well . . . you're wrong."

"You deny you left the cottage at exactly"— Abbisanti checked a little notepad he had flipped open on the white tablecloth, next to his empty plate—"one-eleven A.M.?"

"Dad, I think I'd like to have a lawyer present."

"A lawyer!" Mr. Washburn rolled his eyes in annoyance. "Here we go! What for, Jack? What is it this time? Let me guess. You mooned a bunch of old ladies. No. You went joyriding and totaled the car? What? What crazy stunt—"

"It was more serious than that," Mr. Abbisanti said. "A lot more serious."

"Dad, if I'm going to be interrogated here, then I really think it's best if—"

"He doesn't need any lawyer," Mr. Washburn told Abbisanti angrily. Then to Jack: "Just answer his questions, son, and don't waste our time with any more of that lawyer crap."

"Tell your father where you went, Jack," Mr. Abbisanti said. He waited. "Just tell him where you went, Jackie. Then we can all go about our business. Tell him *where* you went and *what* you did."

Jack's lip was trembling; another tear dripped down his cheek. This time he didn't bother to wipe it away. His hands were in his lap and shaking too hard to risk bringing them out from under the table. The truth was, he wanted to tell his father what he'd done. He wanted to tell and have a good cry about it and somehow have it all be better. Then maybe he could apologize to Martin's dead body and the poor boy could come back to life.

203

But none of that was possible, now was it?

He looked at his father, as if for guidance. That was a joke. But one bit of advice his father had given him did come back to him. It had been on a day when Mr. Washburn had returned from some big financial meeting. His father was in such a good mood that he had played with little Jackie for hours.

Jack was only six at the time. He couldn't understand most of the success story his father had gloatingly recounted. But he did remember the story's punch line. His father had drummed it into him, and it had stayed with him all his life.

In negotiations, whoever talks first, loses, Mr. Washburn had told him. Remember that, son.

And right then . . . it hit him. The detective wouldn't be talking this way unless . . .

Jack stared back at the detective as boldly as he could. "Why don't *you* tell my father what I did," he said.

Abbisanti waited, then glanced at Mr. Washburn, then back at Jack. Staring right into Jack's eyes, he said, "You've got one smart cookie here, Mr. Washburn."

Jack blinked away a fresh tear.

"One smart cookie. Right, Jackie?"

Abbisanti sat back, looking annoyed. "Jack here must have seen me following him that night, because he managed to lose me. So unfortunately I don't know exactly where he went. I know when he came back. That's all. I've got some theories, though. I sure know it was a pretty strange time of night for him to be taking a road trip."

"Where did you go, Jack?" asked Mr. Washburn.

Jack didn't answer. He had come so close to telling. So close! Even though his hands were still shaking, he now brought them out from under the table. He pushed himself up. "This is absurd," he said. "Absurd!" He said it loud enough to turn heads at nearby tables. "What am I? A criminal?"

"You tell *us*, Jack," Abbisanti said easily.

Mr. Washburn held up a hand, giving Abbisanti a warning glance, as if to say, "I'll handle this."

The detective shrugged. He was smiling.

Mr. Washburn turned back to Jack. "I'm invoking the good-behavior clause in your trust fund, son. I'm taking back that money. Because quite frankly, I don't think you're mature enough to handle it. I don't think you've got the character. You're not enough of a man. Now, if at some point in time you show me that you've changed, then I'm willing to reconsider—"

"I don't want your money!" Jack spat out. "I don't want your filthy money."

He was feeling more confident every second. He glared down at his father. "You *dare* talk to me about maturity, character? After you cheated on my mother?"

"Now that's enough!"

Mr. Washburn had turned bright red. He stood up. He was taller than Jack. "Get out," he said coldly. "Get out before I—"

Jack cut him off. "And one more thing, *Dad*. About Jill. She's got more class in her little finger than you've seen in your entire lifetime. You got that?"

Jack pushed his way out of the booth, jostling the table hard enough to slosh the water glasses. He strode out of the restaurant without looking back.

CHAPTER 29

IT WAS QUITE A THRILL, IN A WAY, TELLING HIS father off like that. It was something he'd wanted to do for years. But the excitement faded long before he'd gotten back to campus. And by six o'clock that night, he felt totally drained. The next time he had to face that detective, he knew he'd lose.

The school bell chimed six times. During the chiming, the mill sounded its siren. Jack stood in front of his closet mirror, clumsily tying a double Windsor knot in his school tie as he got ready for dinner. His fingers felt thick, dead.

"Okay," Hunt said. "Let's have it."

Jack whirled. Hunt was standing in the doorway.

He wants the money, he realized.

"Let's have what?" he asked coldly.

"What's going on with you, man? Who put the bug in your brain?"

He wants to keep playing the game, thought Jack as he went back to tying his tie. "Hunt, I'm in no mood, okay? Don't push it. Just stop sending me those whacked-out messages and we'll be friends again. Deal?"

"Deal, except I didn't send you any messages, okay, Looney-Tunes?"

"Get out," Jack said. "I'm serious, Hunt. We've got an understanding, but that's it. You know what I mean?"

"No, as a matter of fact, I have absolutely no idea what—"

"We've got a deal," Jack went on. "And a deal's a deal, am I right? And then—*finito*. That's it."

"Jack, please don't take this the wrong way, but I really think you might want to stop by the infirmary and talk to Mrs. Mack."

"Go to hell, Hunt."

Hunt sighed. "I thought I was already there." He smiled wanly. "I always liked you, Jack, you know that? Which is a big compliment coming from me. 'Cause I don't like too many people. Least of all myself. But if you don't want to be friends anymore . . ."

"That's right, I don't. And you don't need to net me anymore either. I already got the message."

"I'm glad to hear it," Hunt said as he strolled casually out the door.

He was barely out of sight when Jack's console beeped. Twice.

Jack turned slowly toward the machine, the tiny hairs on the back of his neck standing on end.

JUST A LITTLE REMINDER. ONLY THREE SHOPPING DAYS LEFT TILL SUNDAY. HA-HA. AND IF THE MONEY'S NOT THERE . . .

CHAPTER 30

"YOU'RE CLOSING OUT YOUR ACCOUNT?"

"That's right."

"Then you're going to need the approval of an officer."

The teller pushed his check back under the grille. Jack turned and looked at the line of local yokels waiting to see the one fat bald bank officer. He turned back to the teller. "There isn't any way *you* could authorize the withdrawal for me? I'm in kind of a rush. See, this is my only free period during the school day and—"

The teller smiled and shook her head. For a second Jack thought it was a friendly smile. "You preppies," she said, still smiling. "You think you own the world, don'tcha? Expect us to bend all the rules for you, *don'tcha?*" The young bony-faced woman leaned her head closer to the brass grillwork and lowered her voice as if imparting some great secret. "You're going to have to go see the bank officer," she said with mock sweetness.

"Thank you."

Jack took his place on line to see the officer, shifting impatiently from foot to foot as he waited. He kept glancing at his watch. Except his watch was no longer there. He'd pawned it ten minutes ago, for five hundred dollars.

Where he was standing, right near the bank entrance, he was getting hit with blasts of freezing air as customers entered and exited. But Jack was sweating. For one thing, he now knew that Hunt wasn't the blackmailer. Hunt had been practically standing inside his room when the last message was sent.

And then there was the message itself, which hadn't calmed Jack down either. What if he didn't get the money together by Sunday? What then?

He knew what then.

After he cashed out his account, Jack headed back to the dorm, cutting American history. Skipping a class altogether without an excuse—that was worth two cut slips. How many cut slips for murder? Jack wondered idly.

He made ten signs, carefully copying the information over and over.

ROOM SALE
UNBELIEVABLE LOW-LOW PRICES.
EVERYTHING MUST GO!
(CASH ONLY)

He put the notices in all the guys' dorms, advertising the hours for the sale (that afternoon from three till check-in) and his room number. For Whitmanites, the sale continued until lights-out. Jack had some good stuff. A lot of guys had coveted his things for a long time. There were students swarming all over his room, holding up his possessions, yelling out, "How much for this?" and "Can I have this?" and pulling open drawers, and—"What about the underwear,

Jack? That for sale?" Everyone was cackling. Kids were driving hard bargains, too; they were smelling blood.

By quarter of eleven, when Jack finally kicked everyone out, his room looked as if it had been raped. His new neighbor, Stuart, had bought his autographed Superbowl football for ten dollars. That had been particularly galling, but Jack had swallowed his anger and taken the money. Now, as he sat at his desk chair, counting the cash, he could see Stuart tossing the football up and down in his room across the hall. Jack leaned over and kicked the door shut.

Along with his bank account and his Rolex money, the total came to $15,313.29.

Well, he still had the Porsche.

He lay down on his water bed without taking off his clothes or getting under the covers. A first former had bought the water bed, but agreed not to take it till next Monday. The ceiling overhead was splotchy and bare—the parachute had cost a second former twenty-five dollars.

With so much of his stuff gone, the room reminded Jack of the way his first Whitman room had looked, five years ago. The year that Martin had . . .

The Braddington Art Department was housed just outside the main campus gate in a sunny white Victorian house. The place had been bought for the school by a Braddington alumnus who had gone on to make a fortune as a Wall Street corporate raider. That alumnus was now serving time in Club Fed, one of the nation's low-security prisons.

Jack found Jill, as planned, in the back of the large first-floor studio. She was sitting at the potter's wheel, her apron and her face spattered with wet gray clay, a lopsided mess slowly revolving in front of her.

"What do you call it?" Jack asked, smiling. "Don't tell me. It's abstract, right?"

She didn't laugh, or smile, or even answer. She waited until the wheel stopped spinning, then got up, holding her messy hands in the air. She walked over to a long drawing table and kicked at her purple backpack, which was stowed underneath. "Open it," she told him.

He looked at her curiously. There was something different about her, but he couldn't quite figure it out. Then he realized. Her neck was bare. He could see the beautiful recessed spot at the base of her neck. But that meant—

She wasn't wearing her silver pendant.

The sweet-sixteen present from her dad was missing.

"Open it," Jill ordered.

Jack knelt down and unzipped the pack.

"See that white envelope?"

"Yeah, but—"

"Take it."

Jack pulled out the envelope. He could see the money through the thin paper. "I can't take this," he said.

"You're taking it," she said firmly. "It's only seventy-six dollars," she said. There were tears in her eyes. She got back on the wheel. "Don't forget you're supposed to come over for lunch on Sunday," she said, spinning the big heavy wheel with her sneaker. She studied the clay. "Mom hates it when people are late."

Jack nodded, but she wasn't looking at him anymore.

The conversation was over.

*   *   *

That night he got an E-mail message, signed this time. It was from Brooke, saying the gang was expecting him at the dance in the student union. BE THERE—OR ELSE!

Jack didn't go. He thought about going to a movie instead. The student film society showed films every Friday and Saturday night in the rotunda. He checked the schedule. Tonight they were showing a double bill of *Fatal Attraction* and *In Cold Blood*.

Jack spent the night in his room, counting his money.

He hadn't sold the Porsche. Maybe whoever was after him would just take the car and the money and call it square. Then he could hitch back to campus. It would have to do, for now.

At around eight, there was a knock at his closed door. "Jack?"

"Go away," Jack said.

"It's me, Cameron."

"I don't want to talk."

A long silence. He knew Cameron was still at the door.

"Are you okay?" Cameron finally asked.

"I'm fine."

"You don't seem so fine, lately."

Jack waited, staring at the door.

"You're going to have to talk to me sometime, buddy," Cameron said.

Jack felt chills.

Was it Cameron?

"I'm in my room," Cameron said. And at last Jack heard the footsteps walking away. Just as—

His terminal beeped twice.

SEE YOU SUNDAY, JACK.

CHAPTER 31

ON SATURDAY AFTERNOON, JACK WENT TO the gym to work out. He lifted weights, ran some laps, then went to the basketball court and started shooting foul shots. At one point, he sank six buckets in a row, swishing every one. It's my lucky day, he thought.

He was lining up for shot seven when the gym doors opened and the gang strolled in—Hunt, Cameron, Bradford, Dede, and Brooke. They had often played a pickup game of basketball together on rainy Saturday afternoons. Those days were gone. Cameron and Brooke had broken up—apparently for good this time. So had Dede and Hunt. Right now there was zero camaraderie in the air. Just an awful tension.

They gathered around Jack in a loose circle, all in their gym grays, all wearing grim faces. Just then, a pimply first former stuck his head into the gym. He took one look at the circle of students over by the hoop and ducked back out immediately.

Jack dribbled carefully, shot the foul shot. He banged it off the rim. "You broke my streak," he told them.

Hunt snatched the rebound, dribbled a layup, sank it, then turned and tossed the basketball hard at Jack's chest. "Ready to *talk?*"

Jack caught the ball, but it stung. "About *what?*" He tossed it back.

"Jack," Cameron said, in that ever-so-serious voice of his, "some of us would like to know why you've been avoiding us lately."

"Me especially," Brooke told Jack, making exaggerated goo-goo eyes. Then she went back to looking angry.

They were all staring at him, a ring of threatening faces, surrounding him like beasts of prey. And suddenly Jack realized—

"Oh, my God. You're all in this together, aren't you?"

"You bet we are," Dede said.

"Dede," he said, feeling abruptly close to tears. "You, too?"

"We all care about you," she said firmly. She had her thin arms crossed across her slender chest.

Bradford took the basketball and bounced it clumsily with his big hands. Basketball wasn't his sport. He stared at the ball, not looking at Jack. "We think you need help, big guy," he said.

Jack looked from face to face. So that was it. Group therapy. Not group blackmail. But one of these so-called friendly faces . . .

"Okay," he said. "Which one of you is doing it to me?"

"Doing *what*, Jack?" asked Cameron, pushing his glasses back up his nose. Cameron had been right outside his room last night when Jack got that message . . . he'd already ruled out Hunt. That left—

"Brooke? You the one?"

"I certainly hope so, Jack." She flicked her hair back with her hand, fluffing it.

"You're in love with me. Is that the deal?" asked Jack.

Brooke gave him a strange look. "In your dreams, Washburn."

"'Cause you were the one who came after *me,* Brooke. I just want to remind you of that little fact. I know you felt hurt, but you made the first moves, okay?"

There was a stillness in the room now that made Jack's head spin. It took him a moment to realize what he had done.

"Yeah," he said loudly, "you heard right, guys. For those of you who don't know—and I doubt that leaves anyone in this room—Brooke and I fooled around. Brooke, you're a great kisser, I admit. I enjoyed it. But do you really think I deserve to pay like this?"

Cameron lunged for him. Bradford got in between. But Cameron was struggling so hard that even Bradford had trouble holding him back.

"I'll kill you, Brooke!" Cameron shouted. "I'll kill you."

So it wasn't Jack that Cam was going for, after all.

Brooke was holding on to Dede, as if for protection. There were tears in Brooke's dark eyes. "Why'd you have to do that, Jack? Why?"

"You are such an actress," Jack spat out. "Like Cameron didn't know about that! Give me a break, Swanson. You probably told him that same night, just to torture him."

Cameron was bellowing as Bradford pinned his arms behind his back in a full nelson, which was an illegal move, but where was the ref?

"Sounds to me like Cam didn't know, Jack," said Hunt.

Jack grabbed a fistful of Hunt's gray shirt. "You can't stop running your mouth, can you, Lowry?"

Hunt had both hands on Jack's wrist, trying to pull his hand off.

"Why don't you tell Cameron about *your* little make-out sessions with Brooke," Jack snarled. "Huh, Hunt? How about it? That's right, guys. While he was supposed to be going out with Dede, he and Brooke were sucking face! Tell him, you little piece of slime!"

He had shoved Hunt all the way back to the gym wall. He banged him against the wall with all his might, but the wall was matted, so it wasn't an effective move. Hunt bounced off the mat, pushing him away. There was a sneer on his face. He came after Jack, slapping at him, snapping his fingers in his face.

Jack cocked his fist. This time Bradford was busy trying to calm Cameron. There was no one to stop him. Jack landed a punch right on Hunt's jaw.

Hunt's head snapped back. It felt like Jack had broken his hand. He glanced down at it. It was bleeding.

Hunt licked his lips, then spat out a glob of blood and at least one tooth. Then he charged at Jack and they went down together, wrestling and punching each other like mad. Jack ended up on top. He had a hold of Hunt's long dark hair and was banging Hunt's head down onto the gym floor again and again. Everyone was screaming, their voices echoing through the gym. Jack might have been screaming himself, he didn't even know.

Then someone pulled him off—Bradford? Jack was only on his feet for a second when Cameron attacked him—and they were fighting again. Cameron knocked him down. Jack felt a punch land right on his ear, so that his whole head rang. Old instincts died hard. The feel of his back against the floor was electric. He struggled to get up with all his might. He was getting there, too, but then he caught a glimpse of Hunt on all fours, struggling to his feet as well. Jack lost his concentration, and Cameron dragged him back down to the gym floor again. He saw a fist smash right into his face.

His vision blurred. But he was vaguely aware of Brooke and Dede, trying to pull Cameron off him. He rolled away—right into a sneaker that caught him hard in the stomach.

Hunt was kicking him. And Cameron had pulled away from the screaming girls and was coming for him as well. Jack covered his face with his hands as the blows landed. His back, his head, his gut . . .

When the blows finally stopped, he lay still for a long time, wondering if he was alive, and half hoping he was dead.

He moaned softly, but barely any sound came out. He opened his eyes. Bradford was standing over him. Cameron and Hunt were both on the floor on either side of him, apparently where Bradford had tossed them. Bradford was bellowing at everyone. No one else spoke.

After a while Bradford stopped shouting and stepped away from Jack. He offered Jack a hand. Jack didn't take it. He slowly got to his feet. Which wasn't easy. He could feel the blood flowing out of his nose. He gently felt his face, half expecting to find missing features. There was a sticky wetness trickling down from his old forehead scar. A kick had opened the old wound again.

Jack lifted his gray T-shirt and mopped his face with it.

"You okay?" Bradford asked him.

He didn't answer. He looked around the room. He could barely see, thanks to the blood seeping down into his eyes. Dede was silently weeping. Brooke had her hand over her mouth. Jack raised a hand weakly in the air. "Just stay away from me. All of you. Just stay away."

It was unnecessary advice.

No one made a move to come near him as he walked shakily out the door.

Fifteen minutes later Jack sat alone in the steam room, enveloped in hot mist—and fear. He ached all over, inside and out. He kept mopping at his face with his towel, and even in the mist he could see the fresh dark stains made by his blood.

The glass door opened.

A figure entered.

Thanks to the thick clouds of steam, Jack couldn't be sure who it was. . . .

Then he saw—

Bradford.

"I think we should talk," Bradford said.

The big guy towered above him. Clouds of steam swirled around his massive head, clearing and unclearing.

"It's time," Bradford said menacingly.

"Bradford," Jack said weakly. "It can't be you."

"I thought you'd never guess," Bradford said.

CHAPTER 32

"OH, GOD!"

Jack felt like he'd been kicked in the stomach one more time. Only this blow hurt more than all the others. He moved away from Bradford, sliding across the tiled platform. "Bradford . . . you were the only one I could trust."

"Jack," Bradford said. "I think you're crazy. I'm serious, man. I think you just totally lost your marbles. I never thought I'd see the day, but it's here."

It took Jack a moment to process that. "You mean . . . you're not the one . . . ?"

"The one *what*?"

"Who's blackmailing me?"

Bradford stared at him a long time. Then he took off his white towel and laid it down carefully on the platform next to Jack. He sat down heavily. "Okay, I'm ready. Shoot. I want to hear it all, Jack."

Jack watched his face closely as he told him about the messages he'd been getting. Then he grinned with sudden relief. "Bradford, it really isn't you, is it?"

"No, it's not."

It was like having a lost dog come running back to you. He loved Bradford, he really did.

"That's the first piece of good news I've heard in a long time," he told him.

"Good. So you ready to talk?"

"I killed Martin," Jack said. He said it quickly, without even thinking. Blurted it right out.

Bradford's face showed no expression. "I know that, Jack."

"You know?"

"Well . . . I figured."

"H-how?"

"I got a late start, driving up to Hunt's mom's that Friday. On my way off campus, I ran into Martin. He was babbling about how you invited him up to the chalet. He was very nervous and excited. Like a yip-yip dog. I thought he was going to wet his pants."

"Jesus. But then . . . why didn't you—"

"Say anything? I'm still your friend, Jack. You seem to have forgotten that."

Jack let his head hang back against the warm wet tiles. "Yeah. So what do you think about your old captain now, Bradford?"

Bradford didn't answer. Didn't have to. "I'm not going to tell anyone, Jack. But that's as far as I can go."

Jack nodded.

Hands on knees, Bradford rose heavily to his feet. "C'mon."

"Where are we going?" Jack asked.

"Back to my room. I think I have a way we can find the scuzz who's E-mailing you."

"But—"

"I told you, Jack. You're still my friend, no matter what you did. Now let's go."

Back in Bradford's room, Jack watched him boot up his computer.

"Have a seat," he told Jack, pulling up a chair next to the console with his big bare foot.

Jack sat down gratefully. His body felt broken.

Bradford was looking at him. "You need to go to the infirmary?"

"Nah."

"You look like death warmed over, pal."

"I don't know why. Usually my body perks right up after getting kicked in the head."

Bradford considered him a moment longer. Shrugged. Then turned back and studied the screen. He reached down into the messy pile of books and papers that cluttered the floor at his feet. He pulled out his manual on the school's computer system, plus the Internet instructions. "Open my desk drawer and hand me my glasses, would ya, Jack?"

"Your what?"

Bradford just held out his hand, wiggling his fingers to indicate "gimme."

Jack found the leather glasses case. "I didn't know you wore glasses."

"I only do it in private."

"Bradford, you're vain."

"No, I'm ugly."

"That's not true."

"Tell it to Dede."

"Bradford, maybe it's time—"

"Don't even try to shrink me, Jack. I'm too big." He snorted at his own joke.

"Well . . . she doesn't know what she's missing," Jack said.

Bradford nodded by way of thanks. "Who knows your password, Jack? Anyone?"

"Everyone, basically. My password is Jack."

"Good thinking. That's really hard to guess, now isn't it?"

"Guess nothing. I have it taped to the side of my computer."

Bradford gaped at him over the tops of his glasses. "What's the matter with you? You can't remember your own name?"

"I wrote it down and stuck it up there the day I picked my password. I wasn't worried about getting blackmailed back then. Anyway, what's the difference?"

Bradford didn't answer. He peered through his glasses at the green screen. "You know, Jack, there's no guarantee that the person who's sending you these messages is inside the school."

"There isn't? But wait a minute. I also got something—this record of Martin's—somebody shoved it under my door, so—"

"That was Hunt."

"It was!"

"Yeah. I got that much out of him by nearly breaking his neck. He found it in Rucker's room after his mom cleaned the place out. Thought it'd be a funny gag to slip it to you. You know Hunt. But he's not the E-ster."

Bradford nodded at the screen. "This is the log of school messages from the past week."

"How did you get that?"

Bradford gave him a look. "I'm not *supposed* to be able to call it up, Jack. It's called hacking, you *ever* hear of that?"

"I'm impressed."

Bradford moved his white mouse over the gray rubber mouse pad, clicking on a column. "Here we go," he said to himself.

Jack moved closer. He didn't know what he was expecting to see. The blackmailer's face? Instead, all he saw were numbers. "What's that?"

"Electronic destinations. To and from."

Bradford found a pencil and copied down a number: 0891.

"That's it?"

"That's the terminal we're looking for."

Bradford started typing. Frowning. Cursing. Jack knew enough to wait quietly and let the master work.

"Zero-eight-nine-one," Bradford said finally. "That doesn't sound like a student terminal."

"So we're looking at someone outside of Braddington?" He was thinking of only one name: Abbisanti.

"Off campus, anyway," Bradford said. More cursing. "Okay, Jack," he said finally, "you better get out of here and let me work. Get some rest. I'll nail this sucker, I promise you that."

Jack felt so grateful, he wanted to cry. "You're the best, Knox."

Bradford had returned to his menu screen. He didn't answer. And as much as Jack trusted Bradford at that moment, he couldn't help glancing over his shoulder at Bradford's terminal number. It was a relief to see it: 5827.

"Jack?"

Bradford was staring at him. Jack reddened. Had he seen him checking?

"I'm coming with you tomorrow," Bradford said. "For the drop."

"No, you're not."

Bradford didn't answer, which Jack knew was Bradford's way of settling—and winning—the argument.

"Hang loose, man," Bradford told him as Jack edged toward the door. "We're going to get you out of this."

If only Jack could believe that.

CHAPTER 33

THAT EVENING, JACK SIGNED OUT FOR THE weekend and drove back to Blueberry Hill. Gotcha, Bradford, he told himself. Because if there was one shred of pride he had left, he could only hang on to it by taking care of this mess himself.

His heart was pounding the whole trip. It was terrifying—returning to the scene of the crime. Everything looked the same. It was as if he were returning not just to the place, but the time. And whenever he glanced in the rearview mirror, he was afraid he'd see Martin in the backseat, grinning at him.

He passed the wooden sign with the hand, pointing right: BLUEBERRY HILL.

He drove up the hill, following the quaint little signs to Chalet 19.

The lights were on.

Jack looked at the wooden sign about three times, making sure it was his chalet. Then he parked the car at the very beginning of the drive, closing the door quietly. He tracked through the thick snow. As he stood on the porch listening he heard movement inside.

It was him.

Jack slipped the key into the lock, turned quietly, then burst into the room. He didn't have any other plan. Instinctively, he felt that it might be nice to surprise someone else for a change. . . .

In the middle of the living room stood a craggy-faced man with a bushy mustache. His neighbor from up the hill.

He was holding a VCR. Jack's father's VCR. He was staring at Jack, slack-jawed.

Jack stared back, his chest heaving. He had never felt such horror and hatred in his life. It was more than he'd ever felt for Martin. At least with Martin his grudge against Jack was personal. But this man had tortured him just for—

"Hi, there," the man finally said.

Leaving the door open, Jack moved slowly into the room. The man made a sick attempt at a smile. "I was just borrowing the VCR . . . for the night, so my wife and I could rent a video."

It was as if there were loud static crackling in Jack's brain. He couldn't understand a word the man was saying. Because he was remembering something the man's wife had said, when Jack was hiding behind their living-room curtains. The guy was in *computers.* So he'd seen Jack that night in his chalet after all. He'd become suspicious, somehow figured it out—

"Look," Jack said, taking out the thick manila envelope that he used to store the cash. "I brought the money. I'm going to give it to you. But if you ever bother me again, I swear to you, I'll kill you. It's that simple. Okay?"

He kept jabbing the envelope at the man. Finally the guy put down the VCR. His eyes were dancing.

"You understand?" Jack said harshly. "We got a deal?"

ERIC WEINER

The man nodded as he reached for the envelope.

For a moment they were both holding the envelope, and glaring at each other across it. Then the man pulled it out of Jack's hand.

"Is it all here?" the man asked casually. He was undoing the metal clasp. He peered inside.

"Sure," Jack lied. And then—something about the way the man was looking at the money made him add, *"All five thousand."*

And then, time stood still for a second as they stared at each other.

"Good," the man finally said, giving him a smile.

Jack smiled back. But he felt like his brain was splitting in two. So this wasn't the blackmailer after all! And suddenly the words seemed to vomit out of him. He was screaming at the man, calling him every name he could think of. He shoved the man back with both hands. The man looked terrified. Then he tried to make a run for it, dodging past Jack toward the front door.

Jack caught him, clapping two hands down hard on the back of the man's thick black sweater. He threw him back into the room.

The man windmilled his arms as he stumbled toward the stone fireplace and—

An explosion of blood spurted everywhere.

The left side of the moose's antlers were sticking out of the man's throat.

CHAPTER 34

"HELLO? MR. WASHBURN? *HELLO?* ANYBODY home?"

Old dame Dobb was sticking her scraggly white-haired head in through the open door of the chalet. "Hello?"

"It's me, Mrs. Dobb," Jack called from the top of the stairs.

"Oh, Jack! Oh, my goodness." Mrs. Dobb put a hand to her throat. "You scared me! I saw the lights, you see. And I knew—oh, let me just catch my breath—I knew there wasn't supposed to be anyone here tonight. And then the front door was open. Your father didn't tell me you'd be staying here this week-end. . . ."

"My father didn't know."

Mrs. Dobb frowned, then clucked her tongue and wagged a finger. "Oh now, Jack, I hope you're not misbehaving again."

"Again?"

She had her coat on, unzipped. Keys in her hand. She jangled the keys. "Naughty naughty."

Jack didn't smile.

"Is she here, too?"

"That's none of your business."

"Oh, now, Jack, come on now. It's me. We're friends, aren't we?"

Jack moved down a step. "I thought we were."

"Of course we are. Oh, Jack, listen . . . while I've got you, maybe you can help me . . . there's a little matter of some money due."

"Is there?" Jack started moving slowly down the stairs, keeping his right hand at his side.

He was thinking about what Bradford had said.

Someone outside the campus . . .

Mrs. Dobb was here that night. Who knew what she had seen? And Bradford had admired her computer setup. What had he called her machine? A screamer.

"Yes, I was going over my records, Jack, and—"

Mrs. Dobb gasped, almost choking. Her knees buckled. She had just noticed the man who still hung from the moose's antlers. One of his long arms had draped across the mantel. The man's eyes were open. His blood was pooling beneath him on the stone hearth.

She turned back to Jack. He raised his right hand. The hand that held his father's gun. "It's you, isn't it, Mrs. Dobb?"

She stammered. She couldn't even speak she was so guilty.

"Computers are your new hobby, eh, Mrs. Dobb?"

He fired.

CHAPTER 35

"BRIDGE! BRIDGE!" YELLED COACH MICHAELS.

Jack was on his back as Dennehy painfully ground the sharp plastic chin strap of his helmet into his sternum, pressing down with all his weight and strength.

"Bridge, Jack! Bridge!"

When you bridged, you used your neck strength to try to arch your back off the mat—and keep from getting pinned. Jack was straining every tendon. In that position, with his head upside down, Jack caught the agony on Coach Michaels's face, which appeared to be upside down as well. And past him, Jack could see the big smile on Martin's face in the front row.

Jack could feel the ref frantically slipping his hand under his back. Screaming, Jack lifted first one shoulder, then the other. If the ref didn't find enough space between shoulders and mat, the match was—

The ref's hand slapped the mat. Over!

The Andover crowd roared. As . . .

The ref slapped the mat again. And again. And again.

Jack moaned groggily, slowly coming back to consciousness. Someone was pounding on his door. A dream—the nightmare—again. He sat up, feeling shooting pains in his head, back, chest—

Then he picked up the digital clock and held it right up to his blurry eyes, staring at the red numbers. 12:30. Impossible! He had set it for eleven. He didn't remember *why* he had set it for eleven, but he remembered setting it and—

He pressed down on the button that was labeled ALARM. The clock showed its alarm setting: 11:00. With a little red dot. Which stood for—

P.M.

He threw the clock hard against the wall.

Then he remembered the knocking at the door. "Hello?"

"Jack?"

"Who is it?"

"Nicky Markham."

Who?

Jack stalked to the door and flung it open. He had to look down, the boy was so short. A first former. Jack recognized him by face but not by name.

"I'm sorry to bother you, Jack," the boy said shyly. Like most young Whitmanites, the boy regarded Jack with obvious awe.

Not for long, thought Jack. Not for long.

"There's a girl on the phone for you. Says it's urgent. She said if you were sleeping, I should wake you up for sure."

Jack rubbed his face with both hands. "Okay. Thanks."

He was about to close the door.

"Aren't you going to get it?" the boy asked.

"What? Oh, yeah. Of course I am. Thanks."

Jack headed for the stairs.

Then he remembered why he had set the clock for

eleven, and he started taking the stairs two and three at a time.

There was a crowd in the common room watching TV. The pay phone's receiver was dangling. Jack had to talk really loud to be heard over the noise.

"Jack?"

"Jill?"

"Did you forget about lunch?"

"I'll be right there!"

"Everyone's waiting."

"I know, I'm sorry, I—"

He was going to explain what happened, about the alarm clock, but the real excuse froze his tongue. He'd been up half the night burying bodies and cleaning up the mess. You couldn't ask for a better excuse than that.

The tiny dining room of the Marshacks' house was about the size of Martin Rucker's old single. The floor tilted, and the worn sideboard across from Jack was at a slight angle. Or maybe it's just that my brain is shot, thought Jack.

"This roast beef is delicious, Mrs. Marshack," he said.

"What?"

"I say, 'This roast beef is delicious!'"

"Don't be afraid to shout," Jill told him. "It's the only way they can hear you."

"I know!" Jack shouted.

Jill laughed. "You don't have to shout at *me*, Jack."

Mrs. Marshack passed him the plastic bowl of mashed potatoes, which were totally tasteless. Jack had almost gagged on his first serving and had to work really hard to force them all down. "Have some more!" Mrs. Marshack said, cheerfully plunking the bowl down in front of him.

She was a tall woman, like Jill, but she had become quite stout. Except for her bad arm, that is, which was thin and atrophied. It hung straight down at her side. Jack was having trouble keeping his eyes off it.

"Jill says you wrestle," Mr. Marshack shouted at him.

"That's right!" he shouted back.

"Last night?" Mr. Marshack repeated.

"That's right!" Jill shouted it out for him.

Mr. Marshack nodded. "I *thought* wrestling season was over. You know our Walter wrestled."

Jack nodded across the table at Jill's brother. Redder hair, and lots of freckles, but the resemblance to Jill was obvious. Walter was eyeing him coldly. "What weight class?" Jack shouted, straining his voice.

Jill touched his arm. "You don't have to shout at Walter. He hears fine. It's James who . . ."

Jack felt his stomach turn with embarrassment. He glanced over at James. He had his head down and was shoveling in the food, apparently content not to be distracted by conversation. Being hard of hearing—that sounded good to Jack at the moment.

Walter was still staring at him. "Jill says you're a millionaire," he said.

"Walter," Jill said. "Be good."

She glanced nervously at Jack. She'd been doing that throughout the meal, throwing him these sideways frantic searching looks. Jack was already coming unglued. He didn't need any more pressure. Besides, it was so absurd, her worrying what he'd think of her family. He had just killed two more people. She didn't owe him any apologies.

"Jack, you like to hunt?" Mr. Marshack roared at him.

"Oh, stop," Mrs. Marshack yelled back. To Jack, she said, "If you don't hunt, you better lie, Jack. Thomas only respects men who shoot moose."

In his mind's eye, Jack saw a moose antler piercing a man's throat, saw blood spurting in all directions, saw—

"Jack, are you all right?" Jill asked him. "You look a little green around the edges."

He was standing, though he didn't remember getting up. He had dropped his napkin, he now saw. It suddenly seemed very important to him to pick up that paper napkin and put it back on the table. But when he bent down, he got very dizzy. "Where's the bathroom?" he asked Jill in a low voice.

"You okay?"

"Uh-huh. I just need—"

"Right here."

She was pointing at a door right off the dining room.

"Oh, uh, is there—someplace"—he lowered his voice further—"more privacy—uh—"

"Upstairs," Jill said, alarmed. "You want me to come with you?"

"Oh, no, no," he said, waving her away. He felt drunk. He climbed the steps heavily. The bathroom was right at the top, its door open. He left it open. He sat on the closed toilet, his head in his hands. After a few moments the dizziness passed. He splashed some cold water on his face and dried it with a pink towel, holding the soft cloth over his eyes for a long time. From down in the dining room, he could hear the Marshack family all shouting out boring lunch conversation. He headed for the steps.

233

But before he reached the steps he saw the open door to Jill's room.

And inside Jill's room . . .

He saw—

CHAPTER 36

THERE WAS A SCHOOL COMPUTER TERMINAL sitting on Jill's small, neat desk. Its cursor was winking, winking.

Jack's heart was beating triple time as he walked slowly down the hall, into her room.

Next to Jill's terminal there was a *Forbes* magazine with a very familiar cover.

Jack picked it up. Flipping through, he found the article.

It was a profile about how successful and filthy rich Jack's banker father was.

There was a note scrawled in the margin:

Jill, Doll—

Just remember. It's just as easy to marry a rich man as a poor one.

—Walt

ERIC WEINER

Jack felt like his scalp was burning. He sat down at the terminal. The computer was in word-processing mode, though the screen was blank. He hit escape.

SAVE DOCUMENT Y/N?

He typed N.

EXIT WORD PROCESSING Y/N?

Y.

The screen shimmered as the main menu reappeared.

Up near the top was the terminal number.

0891.

CHAPTER 37

"JACK?"

Jack nearly fell over in his chair.

Jill was standing at the door. She pressed the dimmer switch, turning on the light.

"Is anything wrong?" she asked.

The words gurgled out of him. "I—I don't believe it—I—"

"Jack?"

He stood up, gesturing mutely at the magazine on her desk.

"Oh, God," she said, when she saw where he was pointing. She blushed. "You saw that?"

"Yes, I saw it." It was so hard to talk.

"Oh, Jack—that's Walter for you," Jill said. "From the day I met you, he's been teasing me about how he wants me to marry you and make the whole family rich, but—"

"I'll bet he does."

"Oh, Jack, don't take it that way, he's only joking."

She had put a hand on his chest. He backed away from it hard, shoving into the desk, rocking the computer back and forth. The computer, where— He pointed. "There!"

She looked at the screen. "What?"

The fury he was feeling—it was beyond anger. It was white heat. She was still pretending! He started toward her. "Why you *lying*—"

"Jack, I don't know what—"

His fist shot up.

She cringed, terrified, but he turned and punched the wall. He put his fist right through the cheap plasterboard.

"Jack!"

"'Don't do it, Jack!'" he mimicked. "That's what you said. But you were already planning to blackmail me, weren't you? Weren't you!"

"I don't know what you're—"

"Or was that Walter's idea? It was, wasn't it?"

"No, Jack, you're—"

"Oh, God. Now I get it. It's worse than that, isn't it? Martin was in on this with you, wasn't he? That's why you didn't want me to kill him!"

"Jack, you're out of your—"

"Your terminal Jill!" He clutched his head. "The messages are coming from *your terminal!*"

"What? That's impossible! I—"

Jack swept the computer off the desk, crashing it to the floor. He could still see the cursor winking. He tipped the desk over. And then—

"Jack—what are you—*no!*"

But it was too late. Jack had his hands around her bare neck, and he was choking her.

CHAPTER 38

JACK WAS SCREAMING AS HE SQUEEZED THE life out of her, banging her head back against the wall. Her head must have been hitting the light switch, because the lights in the room kept clicking on and off.

And then, someone smacked him from behind. He went down. As he fell he hit his head hard on the metal corner of Jill's bed frame. He opened his eyes. He wasn't sure. He thought maybe he'd blacked out for a second there. Then he heard the sound of gasping. Slowly he rose to his knees.

He saw Jill, sitting against the wall, holding her throat. Then a foot planted itself on his back and he went down again.

Jill was struggling to get her voice back. She was looking past Jack at—

He turned his head and saw his assailant. Walter. He was on the phone.

Jill raised one hand limply in the air. "Please, no," she begged her brother. "Don't—Walter—"

Don't what? Jack wondered vaguely.

The rest of the Marshack family had trooped up

the stairs, probably come to see why Walter had run out of the room, the deaf old fools. They crowded into the doorway with horrified faces.

"Don't worry!" Walter was shouting at them. "Don't worry! I just called the cops!"

Jack was sitting at a battered metal desk in the tiny offices of the Braddington police, waiting for them to question him. He wished they would talk to him soon. Left alone, he just kept remembering.

Remembering all those times that Martin had knocked at his door, needing someone to talk to.

And most of all, remembering that one very last time.

He'd never told Jill about that time.

It was the night Martin hanged himself.

It was late at night. Maybe two A.M. Jack had an exam the next day. A Latin final. Martin came to the door and knocked. Jack told him to go away. He had the door locked, too. Martin started scratching at the door like some little animal. Begging. Pleading. Weeping. Saying he was going to kill himself. Martin had never said *that* before.

And Martin was saying Jack was the only one who could save him. But . . .

Jack wouldn't let him in.

"I wouldn't let him in," he said aloud.

"What's that?" Across the room, a beefy cop looked up from the papers on his desk. "You say something?"

Jack ignored him.

That's how it had all started. That night.

If only . . .

Jack began to weep.

Fifteen minutes later two investigators sat down to

have a little talk with Jack. They seemed surprised when Jack waived his right to an attorney. They made him repeat it three times, then sign a paper. Then they spent another ten minutes trying to get the tape recorder running. When they were finally ready, Jack confessed to all three murders. But he stressed Jill's role as hard as he could.

He was booked and put in a holding cell. He had only one request, that they let him know when they'd arrested Jill.

Jill was arrested later that night. He saw them lead her past his cell, one cop on either side, Walter and her parents hurrying behind. Jack shouted her name. She turned.

One glance. That was all they got. But the look she gave him was full of hurt and innocence. She was still pretending. She still wouldn't admit what she'd done.

Jack started shaking the bars and screaming like a wild animal. Every curse he could think of. Then he collapsed onto the metal cot.

Jill.

He couldn't believe it—couldn't believe she would betray him like that.

It felt like a knife in the heart.

E P I L O G U E

IT WAS ONE WEEK LATER THAT THE LAST OF
the blackmailer's E-mail messages showed up on
Dean Schmidt's computer terminal.

This last message was by far the longest.

DEAR ESTEEMED DEAN, the message began. PLEASE
VOUCHSAFE ME A FEW MINUTES OF YOUR TIME.

The message was from a senior in Whitman dorm.
The boy wrote that he was about to go off on a weekend trip with Jack Washburn and Jill Marshack. They
were going to go to a Vermont community known as
Blueberry Hill. The boy wrote that he had reason to
fear for his life. Therefore he was taking the precau-
tion of planting some Internet messages in the
school's system and cuing them up to the time/date
stamp.

I'M LISTING MY MESSAGES AS COMING FROM JILL
MARSHACK'S TERMINAL. IF THIS CAUSES JACK AND
JILL NO SMALL AMOUNT OF GRIEF, SO MUCH THE
BETTER. FOR YOU SEE, IF THEY READ THESE MES-
SAGES, THEN MY WORST SUSPICIONS WILL HAVE
COME TRUE, AND I'LL BE DEAD BY THEIR HANDS.

IF, ON THE OTHER HAND, I COME BACK FROM THIS LITTLE OUTING ALIVE, I WILL ERASE THESE MESSAGES.

SO, IN CONCLUSION, RESPECTED DEAN, IF YOU ARE READING THESE WORDS, THEN PLEASE KNOW WITH UTTER CERTAINTY THAT I HAVE MET WITH FOUL PLAY.

WITH SINCERE RESPECT AND ADMIRATION,

MARTIN RUCKER

It was Martin's last message.

Weeks after his own death and his own funeral, Martin Rucker had finally breathed his last breath.

Eric Weiner has written numerous young adult thrillers and has also written for children's television shows such as *Ghostwriter*, *Eureeka's Castle*, and *Gullah Gullah Island*. He lives in Manhattan with his wife and son, and this is his first novel for HarperPaperbacks.